# BLOOD & THUNDER

**by Angela Roquet**

*Blood Vice*
Blood Vice
Blood and Thunder
Blood in the Water
Blood Dolls
Thicker Than Blood
Blood, Sweat, and Tears
Flesh and Blood
Out for Blood

*Lana Harvey, Reapers Inc.*
Graveyard Shift
Pocket Full of Posies
For the Birds
Psychopomp
Death Wish
Ghost Market
Hellfire and Brimstone
Limbo City Lights (short story collection)
The Illustrated Guide to Limbo City

*Spero Heights*
Blood Moon
Death at First Sight
The Midnight District

*Haunted Properties: Magic and Mayhem Universe*
How to Sell a Haunted House
Better Haunts and Graveyards

*other titles*
Crazy Ex-Ghoulfriend
Backwoods Armageddon

# BLOOD & THUNDER

BLOOD VICE BOOK TWO

## ANGELA ROQUET

VIOLENT SIREN PRESS

# BLOOD AND THUNDER

Copyright © 2017 by Angela Roquet



www.angelaroquet.com

Cover Art by Rebecca Frank

Edited by Chelle Olson of Literally Addicted to Detail

ISBN: 978-1-951603-18-2

For Paul and Xavier,

who make my world go round.

# Chapter One

Sometimes, when working a particularly shitty shift, I fantasized about what my life might have been like if I'd been a vampire a few hundred years ago. If my sire hadn't been a total asshat—or dead. I imagined him showing me a good time, somewhere like London. He'd be independently wealthy, and by some other means than running a brothel. I'd wear a ruffled dress, and he a fancy suit with long coattails and a top hat. We'd go dancing, and then relieve a local doctor of his bloodletting collection. The night would conclude with us settling down in a gothic crypt, where he'd gladly answer my every obscure question.

But, unfortunately, I died in the twenty-first century.

There were no ruffled dresses or coattails here. No fancy crypts. My sire was a prick, and now he was *dead* dead. And I had no one to answer the million questions ping-ponging around inside my head along with all these distracting fantasies. Oh. And now that I was one of the undead, I *always* got the shit shifts. Tonight was no different.

I hated running DUI checkpoints. Traffic was backed up down Olive Boulevard, more funneling in off the 141 ramps. The heat of idling engines paired with the sweltering August air was wreaking havoc on my hair and skin. The pits of my uniform were damp, and my legs itched under the thick, brown pants. At least it was dark. Of course, now that I slept like the dead while the sun was up, it was *always* dark.

The night had yielded a handful of sloppy drunks, and one unfortunate bachelorette party that had tried to win over the only gay officer on the force by flashing him. Now that I worked with the K9 unit, I was, thankfully, no longer subjected to the worst of the catcalling and bribery tactics. I simply had to walk Mandy, my werewolf partner moonlighting as a police dog, around any vehicle pulled in for additional questioning.

It was an easy gig, though unbearably mind-numbing. Like most of the rookie tasks we were assigned. Mandy constantly nagged me to push Langford, the new captain I was under, for meatier jobs. She wanted something she could sink her teeth into. Literally. I couldn't afford to tell her how badly I wanted that, too. And I didn't have the heart to tell her that day would never come.

We had to be careful if we wanted to make this last. The circus act we were pulling off was unheard of. Vampires and werewolves living on the fringes of the supernatural society weren't supposed to draw attention. The more eyes, the more risk of exposure. And House Lilith didn't do warnings. Assassinations and executions were more their style—at least, that's what I'd heard from my very limited sources. It made my occupation difficult to manage on so many levels.

Mandy and I couldn't risk doing anything worthy of praise, anything that might make the local newspapers or television stations take an interest in us. That, too, could draw the wrong kind of attention. If Mandy ever bit someone, there was a possibility that it could be deemed unnecessary roughness. There was the chance the suspect would convince a jury they were innocent and demand that Mandy be put down. And heaven forbid she ever get injured on the job.

If a vet sedated her, she'd shift back to her human form. Even if they let her remain conscious for an exam, any half-baked vet would figure out soon enough that she wasn't some rare, mixed-breed dog. Right now, we were fudging her papers with the help of a doctor Mandy knew in Spero Heights, some backwoods town in the Ozarks teeming with all sorts of strange things I didn't even want to know existed.

"Earth to Skye. Come in, Officer Skye." The walkie-talkie clipped on my uniform crackled as Collins' melodious voice sang through it, and I was ripped out of my nineteenth-century London daydream.

I stopped and gave Mandy's leash a gentle pull—the lightest tug imaginable. She growled under her breath and turned her black, wolfy face up to glare at me. We were still working out her job expectation issues with the K9 unit. At least she didn't show her ass too much around the other officers.

I huffed an annoyed sigh before tossing my blond ponytail over my shoulder and pressing a button on my walkie. "I'm here, Collins. What do you need?"

"We're pulling one in, but Ricker and Yogi are still working over the last car. Wanna bring Star down to do a quick trunk sniff?" he asked.

"We'll be right there." I lifted an eyebrow at Mandy. "Lead the way, Princess Pea."

Mandy groaned and grumbled as we turned around and headed back up Olive Boulevard. The white letters spelling out *POLICE* on her ballistic vest glowed in the dark. I knew she hated wearing it in this heat, but it helped disguise the fact that she was no German Shepherd. It also made me feel a tiny bit better about dragging a teenager into my dangerous line of work. Mandy was barely eighteen. We'd celebrated her birthday just the month before, with fireworks and a backyard barbeque, and the small handful of people who knew our darkest secrets.

As we slipped between a pair of cars being flagged through the barricades cutting across Olive, disgruntled drivers shouted through open windows. Someone wanted to know how much longer this was going to take. Someone tried to argue how unconstitutional checkpoints were. Someone called me a bitch. I ignored them all.

The cherries on top of Collins' cruiser flickered over the

road, marking the entrance to the lane blocked off for the lucky few chosen for further inspection. Four officers manned the flow of traffic, while Collins and his partner Ramirez questioned the drawing winners, occasionally calling in Ricker and Yogi or me and *Star,* Mandy's on-duty name, to be extra thorough.

As Mandy and I approached the second car in line—a yellow station wagon with Kansas plates—the driver's door opened. A lanky man with dirty blond, shoulder-length hair stepped out of the car. He wore a flannel shirt and ragged jeans. Our eyes met briefly, and then his attention was pulled away as the beam of a flashlight flickered across his face.

Officer Max Collins was every warm-blooded, hetero woman's idea of perfection. His chiseled chest filled out the shirt of his uniform as if it had been made for him—or made to be torn off on a stage adorned with poles and piles of cash—and his deep green eyes managed to maintain an air of sensitivity even when they smoldered.

"Hey!" Collins shouted at the flannelled man as he circled the car. "Sir, please remain in your vehicle."

A low growl stirred from Mandy, and before the man could say anything, his attention snapped down to my partner. His pupils swelled as he took in Mandy, and then he was off. He tore past the barricades and stumbled over the median and into oncoming traffic. A horn blared, and headlights washed over him. He threw an arm up over his face without stopping until he dropped off into the ditch on the other side of the road.

Collins was hot on his trail, the beam of his flashlight bobbing against the nest of trees not far off—where the Kurt Cobain doppelganger appeared to be heading.

Mandy barked, snapping me out of my shocked trance. And then we gave chase, too—albeit, more methodically and without blindly rushing into traffic. As we caught up with Collins, I felt a stab of panic in my gut.

What had made this man so terrified of Mandy? Did he know what she was? Or would he have reacted this way to any large dog? What would he do once we took him down? What would Mandy do?

My heart throbbed in my chest, dreading the long list of overwhelming possibilities, and my vision was suddenly painted in shades of red. All except for the man we were chasing.

*Vampire.* He was a fucking vampire. And Mandy knew it. I could tell in the way she dragged me ahead of Collins. We had to reach this guy first, and we needed to do it without human intervention. But what we would do when we caught up with him was the real problem.

The man darted past the halo of a street light and under a buzzing row of power lines. Then he disappeared beyond the trees. I squinted ahead, using the Eye of Blood to suss out the path of least resistance through the woods. Creve Coeur Creek dipped under Olive Boulevard and ran alongside a small clearing before coiling back toward us and succumbing to the trees and brush.

My guess was that our suspect would try to cut through the woods long enough to lose us and then cross the clearing and the creek. Collins seemed to agree. He pointed toward the clearing with his flashlight and spared me a quick glance.

"Chase him back this way. I'll cut him off when he comes out the other side." He rubbed his free hand over his forehead and sprinted away from me before I could reply.

I pressed my lips together and ushered Mandy through the brush and bramble outlining the trees. Then I bent down and reached for the leash hook on her collar. I pulled her face in toward mine, directing her eyes away from her quarry and gave her a sharp look.

"We have to make sure he escapes," I said under my breath. "Do you understand?"

Mandy yipped and tugged away from me, but I held firm to her collar.

"This is important," I said through clenched teeth. "If he's caught and held by the human police, House Lilith will hold us responsible."

Mandy grumbled, but she nodded in understanding.

Satisfied, I unhooked her leash. She sniffed the ground as I gazed through the trees, assessing the best way to cut off the vampire before he reached the clearing where Collins would be waiting.

I projected my concentration ahead, weaving it through the thick summer foliage. Leaves rustled, and twigs snapped, and the vampire's breath hitched as he stumbled over a fallen tree trunk.

"There. That way." I pointed south of his location. Hopefully, we could push him north and away from Collins.

Mandy rushed through the woods ahead of me, but I followed closely behind, my blood vision easing my navigation. I couldn't see the creek where it bent around the northern tip of this patch of woods, but I knew it was there. From the higher vantage point atop Olive Boulevard, I'd seen enough to know what needed to be done.

Mandy's growl urged me to hurry, and I doubled my pace again when I heard the vampire hiss. I pulled the can of pepper spray from my belt and tagged a couple of trees before slipping through the brush to where Mandy had cornered our target. They stood frozen, glaring at each other in a tight span of tall grass illuminated by the moon shining through a gap in the canopy. The Kurt lookalike hissed at me next.

"Quiet," I snapped, taking aim at his eyes with the can of pepper spray. "This works just as well on vampires. Trust me."

His snarl evaporated. "You know?"

"I *am*," I countered.

"But you're a cop." His confused eyes shifted to Mandy. "And you're working with a werewolf."

I shook my head. "We don't have time to play twenty questions. You have to get out of here."

"Then why did you stop me?" The snarl was slowly returning.

"Because you're going the wrong direction. There's already an officer waiting for you east of here, and the school and residential area beyond that will guarantee a full-blown search party." I pointed north. "The creek cuts through the woods and then dips under 141. Stay in the water until you get at least that far."

Another dog—Ricker's German Shepherd, Yogi, I guessed—bayed not far behind us. The vampire flinched at the sound.

"Go," I whispered, pointing north again. "We'll buy you some time."

As soon as he was out of sight, I made a wide circle, spritzing every third tree with pepper spray. Mandy whimpered and rubbed her nose into the earth before covering her muzzle with both paws. Yogi echoed her sounds of distress as he and Ricker joined us.

"Jesus H. Christ." Ricker coughed and hacked as he waved the end of his flashlight back and forth in front of his face. His uniform wasn't as flattering as Collins', highlighting love handles and the Marlboro baby he'd acquired after he ditched his nasty habit. At least his teeth were whiter these days, and he smelled better. After the initial month of mood swings, he was even pleasant to be around again.

"What the hell, Skye? You find a den of bears out here or something?" he asked in between gasping for air.

"I tried to spray the suspect, but the nozzle on my can must be broken." I shrugged and blinked to clear the tears burning in my eyes. "But hopefully Collins got the guy once he slipped out the other side." I nodded my head east, away from the direction I'd pointed the vampire.

"Let's get out of here." Ricker ambled through the trees and led Yogi past the toxic clearing.

Mandy trailed after them, giving a wolfish snort as she stepped around me. I sighed and glanced north, using my fading blood vision to see how far the vampire had made it. He was almost to the creek. He'd be long gone before anyone ventured that far to check.

When I exited the woods, Collins was waiting for me, arms folded across his wide chest. Mandy sat at his feet, an equally cross expression on her furry face. Collins pointed his flashlight in my eyes.

"What happened?" he asked, his voice thick with accusation.

I swallowed and pushed the end of his flashlight down. "My pepper spray malfunctioned."

"Why did you even have it out? That wasn't part of our plan." He pulled the flashlight out from under my hand and pointed it at my face again. I squinted against the harsh light and grunted my offense.

"*Our* plan?" I said, folding my arms to match his. "*We* didn't make a plan. There was no time for that. Ma—*Star* and I caught up to the suspect. I pulled my pepper spray, but the nozzle wouldn't work, and the guy took off."

"Why didn't Star follow him?" Collins' squinty, judgy eyes migrated to my partner. Mandy's ears flattened back against her head as she stared at me.

"The pepper spray must have been too much distraction. I should probably take off early tonight to clean her up," I said.

Collins' lips scrunched together. "Uh-huh."

"I'm sorry." I threw my hands up. "What more do you want from me?"

He finally lowered the flashlight out of my face, but as I turned to head back toward the road, he snatched the can of pepper spray from my belt.

"Hey!" I reached for the can, but not before he had a

chance to depress the nozzle. A stream of bitter fluid shot the ground at my feet. Collins sighed as I grabbed the can away from him.

"I don't get it, Skye," he said, shaking his head as he walked away from me. "I know you've been through a lot, and it can take time getting settled with a new unit, but you've been off your game ever since you came back. You're not even trying anymore. I don't know how long you can keep this up."

I held my breath as I watched him go, the beam of his flashlight dancing across the tall grass as he made his way back to the road. Darkness engulfed me now that my blood vision was gone. It would take longer to retrace my steps to the checkpoint, but that was okay. I was in no hurry.

I hated to admit it, but Collins was right. And I didn't know how long I could keep this up either.

# Chapter Two

Mandy's puffy, bloodshot eyes avoided me on the drive home. She'd shifted into her human form in the back of my new cruiser, within the cocoon of tinted windows, eager to tuck away the magnification of her canine senses. Her tank top and gym shorts were wrinkled, having been stashed in the glovebox. I'd made a petty excuse to Collins about getting her cleaned up after surviving the fog of pepper spray in the woods, and now, after realizing how much it had actually affected her, I felt like an asshole.

"Would it help if I cranked up the AC?" I asked, fiddling with the dials on the dashboard.

Mandy grumbled some noncommittal sound and turned her face away from me to glare out her window.

"I'm hungry," she said, almost accusingly. As if telling her she couldn't take a bite out of the vampire suspect had been a deliberate attempt to deprive her of a tasty snack.

"We could swing by that diner on Delmar."

Mandy snorted. "We always eat there."

"Because it's close and…open 24-hours." My cheeks warmed. "We could drive a little farther into the city if you want. Maybe Denny's or—"

"Forget it." Mandy sighed. "I'll make a sandwich after I wash this crap out of my eyes."

"Sorry," I said, my voice flattened by the weight of guilt. "There was no other choice but to let him go."

"I listened, didn't I?" Mandy snapped. "I don't need a lecture."

"Okay." There was nothing else to say. Nothing she wanted to hear, anyhow. I thumbed a knob on the dash, turning on the radio, and let the crooning classic rock fill the silence while I fretted over our future.

It had been two months since I died, and a month since the department shrink cleared me to return to work. Of course, that had been the easy part. Having a soap opera star for a twin sister had finally worked in my favor. For once.

Laura was good. *Really* good. Her return to Missouri had been inspired by my death, but her lingering stay had more to do with guilt. Guilt over our broken past, mostly. But there was also the unspoken question of what would become of me if she left again. What the hell would I do without her?

Laura filled in for all the daytime activities I couldn't manage anymore. Even signing on with the K9 unit and taking the night shift hadn't been enough to solidify an independent lifestyle. Not during the peak of summer, anyway. As it was, I couldn't even finish out the last hour of my shift.

Sunrise times were slowly extending, but in mid-August, that was only a quarter past six. My shift didn't end until six-thirty. That meant slipping off and meeting up with Laura long enough to trade clothes and vehicles—and give her a rundown of the night so she could work out her script before having donuts with the guys.

*God*, I missed donuts. Laura hated them, always on some diet or another. She pulled off the stunt by doing the stealthy chew-and-spit-into-a-napkin maneuver. And she'd added half an hour to her workouts for fear the minuscule bit of sugar she was consuming would somehow catch up with her if she weren't vigilant. Would somehow destroy her chances of landing an acting gig once she returned to Tinseltown.

She didn't say it out loud, but we both knew the day was fast approaching. By early October, there would be enough time after my shift to make it home and get tucked in before sunset. Of course, I'd need Laura's help again for a few weeks in November to get through the monkey wrench that was daylight savings time. And from mid-February to mid-March. I could pull off the last two weeks of March, but by the first of April, I'd be pretty much fucked until October rolled around again.

All of this was assuming Laura came back after she left for Hollywood. I liked to think that we'd patched up most of our issues, but it had taken ten years and me dying before she returned the first time. And if she landed some prestigious acting role that required months of filming, how could I ask her to give that up for the sake of *my* career?

I had to face reality. No matter how good Mandy and I could have been in the K9 unit, we wouldn't be. And not just because we had to constantly worry about House Lilith. Unless the department's night shift hours were miraculously altered and ran from nine to five, we were shit out of luck.

The realization was slowly breaking my heart. Giving up my new position as a detective had been hard enough, and my fighting spirit had only endured because of the opportunity with the K9 unit. My mother had excelled as both a detective and a K9 officer, and now I could say that I'd failed as both. In record time.

I'd already begun scouring the job listings in the newspaper and online. Factory work, bartending, sorting mail—I'd take just about anything. I couldn't afford to be picky right now. Mandy would have to understand, and she would be welcome to stay with me, even if we weren't working together. The mouthy punk was growing on me.

As if on cue, she turned and blinked her swollen eyes at me across the cab of the cruiser. "What? Do I have a bat in the cave or something?" She ran her hand under her nose and frowned at me.

"You did good tonight," I said, turning my attention back to the street ahead.

"Whatever." The word lacked bite, and I could see her

faint smile in my peripheral as she leaned forward to switch the radio to an alternative rock station.

Blue light glowed through the blinds on the front window when I pulled the cruiser into the driveway. Laura didn't have to be up for another couple of hours. Mandy's brow creased, her curiosity matching my own. We climbed out of the cruiser and made our way up the front walk.

The grass bordering the cracked stretch of concrete hissed against the bottom hem of my brown pants. It needed to be mowed—a task Laura considered beneath her. I wouldn't have minded doing it myself, but mowing in the dark just didn't sound like a very bright idea. I was sure my neighbors would agree. The kid Laura had hired for the task was off to Texas, settling into his dorm at UT Austin before his first semester of college began.

Thinking of college reminded me of Serena, my late partner Will's daughter. She'd be starting at MU soon. She and her mother Alicia were coming over for dinner Monday night. It was sooner than I would have preferred, with the daylight still being problematic, but I knew Serena wouldn't have much time to spare once school began.

Mandy paused at the porch steps, letting me go ahead of

her to unlock the front door. The K9 training had rubbed off on her human habits, and she always seemed to be one step ahead of me. It was a loyal and protective stance that filled me with equal parts pride and discomfort. She was just a girl—a girl I was responsible for. I should have been the one protecting her.

When I pushed open the front door and stepped inside the living room, Laura gasped from her curled up perch on the recliner. Her cell phone was tucked between one shoulder and ear, and she nearly dropped it as she fumbled with a bottle of pink nail polish. She shot a foot out to catch her balance, pressing her freshly painted toes to the edge of the coffee table.

"Jenna's back. I have to let you go," she said into the phone, ending the call before whoever was on the other end had a chance to say goodbye. "You're home early," she said, ignoring the skeptical frown I gave her as I dropped onto the end of the sofa.

"What are you doing up so late? And who was that?"

Laura's face flushed and she bit her bottom lip before glancing at Mandy. "Oh my God. What happened to your eyes?"

Mandy groaned. "I'm going to take a shower," she said, heading for the hallway that led to the room and bathroom she shared with Laura. I stared after her, wanting to apologize again but knowing it would only irritate her.

"Accidental pepper spray incident," I answered, hardening my gaze as I turned back to Laura. "Who were you talking to?"

Her chin lifted, but the blush in her cheeks didn't match her indignant act. "None of your business," she said, which could only mean one person.

"Really, Laura?" I sighed and shook my head. "You deserve better. You're *worth* better." I untied my boots and slipped them off before nudging them under the coffee table. I started on the buttons of my uniform shirt next.

Laura cleared her throat and tightened the cap on her bottle of polish. "So are you off the clock, or am I going in earlier than usual for some reason?"

"We're done for the night," I answered. "It's a three-day weekend, just for you." I stood and pulled my shirt out of my waistband before stripping down to the white tank top I wore underneath. I threw the shirt over my shoulder and headed for my room, eager to discard the brown pants, too. Laura's breath hitched, stopping me as I reached the hallway.

"I'm glad you're home early, and we have a chance to talk," she said, lifting an eyebrow as if in question.

"Let me change into my jammies, and I'll be right back." I hurried off, hoping she hadn't noticed the wince pinching up my face with panic. If she was taking calls from her ex, I knew what it meant.

David Steckleman, the prick I none-too-affectionately called Hollywood, had whisked Laura away to California after our mother's death. It looked as if he were set to do so again. *Over my dead body*, I thought bitterly. Then a soft snort escaped me as I remembered that I *was* dead.

Anger tightened my limbs, and I closed my bedroom door a little harder than necessary. I threw my shirt inside the overflowing hamper between my bathroom and closet and stripped out of my pants and socks before adding them to the heap. Then I located a pair of cotton shorts in a pile on top of my dresser. I hadn't broken Mandy of riffling through my clothes, but she was getting better about not leaving things on the floor at least.

I made a detour into the kitchen, snagging a bag of blood out of the refrigerator before joining Laura in the living room again. I had a feeling the comfort food was going to be necessary for this conversation.

Laura eyed the blood but refrained from making a face. "I've become so desensitized to the sight of gore after the summer I've had with you, I could probably land a role as a slasher film villain."

"There's an idea. It'd be a perfect role to distance yourself from that dying soap opera. I knew it wouldn't last long without you," I added, hoping my suspicion was wrong. But the pained look on Laura's face was all the confirmation I needed. "Laura, he cheated on you!"

"I'm not taking him back," she protested. "Yet."

"Really? Why?" Red throbbed at the edges of my vision. I chomped down on the corner of the blood bag, hoping to stave off my frustration.

"He's offering to double my salary if I return to the show." She bit her bottom lip, and a mischievous sparkle touched her eyes. "He hasn't admitted it, but I heard through a friend of a friend that the network is threatening to drop the show if ratings don't improve this season."

The blood bag crinkled as I sucked it dry, and my fangs extracted with a sharp pop. "Good," I snapped. "He deserves to fall flat on his ass, and you should let him. Besides, I thought you wanted bigger and better roles. I thought you wanted him to cower at your glorious comeback. What happened to that game plan?"

Laura shrugged and pulled her legs up into the recliner, tucking her knees under her chin. She glanced down at her shiny, pink toenails and scraped a fingernail at a smudge of polish on her foot. "I haven't had any other offers. My agent thinks this is my best option right now, too."

"It's been two months. You should give it more time." I tried to keep my voice even and encouraging rather than succumb to desperate whining. "You can do better."

She glared up at me through her lashes. "So could you. Do you think I haven't noticed the shit job listings you've been circling in the paper?"

I took a disheartened breath and licked the blood from my lips. "That's different. I don't have a choice—not if you eventually want to go back to your star-studded life."

"You don't have a choice?" Laura pressed her lips together. "Bullshit. How many times has that FBI agent called you?"

I shook my head and pushed up off the couch, heading for the kitchen. I'd underestimated how much blood I would need. This was definitely a two-bag encounter. Laura stood and followed me, refusing to let up.

"I'm not saying this for my benefit," she said. "Don't you think I would rather you work a boring, safe job like putting together toolboxes in a factory?"

"Then what's the problem?" I yanked open the fridge door and cringed as the hinges protested.

My strength had increased over the past few months, and I was still getting used to it. I wasn't She-Hulk or anything like that. I couldn't lift a car over my head—not that I'd tried to— but I'd definitely surprised myself a few times. It scared me. Not so much the thought of breaking all the things, but the idea that my strength might be another royal scion gift that average vamps didn't have.

Part of me wondered if Roman's persistent calls weren't just to make sure I was behaving and keeping to the shadows. I couldn't bring myself to believe he wanted to work with me again—if what I'd done with him could actually be considered work. I'd served more as a handler for Mandy. It was her coveted tracking skills that Roman had really been after. I was just a useless tagalong that had disobeyed an order to stay behind when he raided the Scarlett Inn's safe house with Blood Vice, the underground vampire police force run by the Duke of House Lilith.

A throat cleared behind me as I stared into the abyss of the refrigerator. "Do you really have to think about it?" Mandy asked. "It's either blood or blood. Hurry up, I'm hangry."

I grabbed a blood bag and moved aside so she could dig out her sandwich fixings. Her eyes were still red, but the swelling around them had gone down. Her wet hair dripped onto the collar of a Metallica tee shirt, one that was actually hers and not mine. Laura had reluctantly taken Mandy to a few garage sales over her birthday weekend, while I'd slept the day away.

The girl had money stashed away—including the two thousand I'd stupidly given her to shift in front of Laura so we could fast-forward through her disbelief. What could I say? I was a sucker for convenience. My loss, Mandy's gain.

Though I couldn't figure out why she was pinching her pennies so tightly. It wasn't like I expected her to help pay for utilities—or even the massive amount of food she could put away in no time at all. And I was even splitting my check with her, right down the middle. It was only fair.

I bit into the second blood bag before turning around to face Laura again. She sat on a barstool at the counter, giving Mandy an apprehensive look as if she weren't sure we should be discussing my tentative career in front of her.

Mandy closed the fridge door and dumped her loot onto the counter before shooting a bored glance at us. "Don't stop bickering on my account." She reached across the counter between Laura and me to grab the loaf of bread.

Duncan, my sister's spoiled Chihuahua, pranced a circle around Mandy's feet, his buggy eyes watching for any stray crumbs that might fall his way. Mandy bared her teeth at him until his scavenger path widened. Once she was satisfied with the distance, she tossed him a slice of turkey, earning a grunt from Laura. The pooch had put on some weight this summer, straying from his usual diet of high-end kibble.

"Okay," Laura said to Mandy as she sat up straighter. "Maybe it's best you're a part of this since it affects you, too."

My throat tightened with panic. I opened my mouth, but nothing came out. Laura was right, and she accepted my defeat with a tight grin. I sniffed at her before biting into my blood bag.

Mandy twisted open a jar of mayonnaise and slicked some onto a slice of bread with a butter knife. "I have exceptional hearing, but who needs it when I live with the two of you?"

"You heard all that?" Laura gave her an apologetic wince.

Mandy licked the butter knife clean before dropping it into the sink. "It's nothing I didn't already know. I'm not stupid."

"But what will you do?" Laura asked.

I pulled my teeth out of the blood bag and swallowed hard. "She doesn't have to do anything. She can stay here as long as she wants. Maybe get her GED online, or…or mow lawns. Hell, she could mow *our* lawn. I'd pay you to do that," I said, turning to Mandy.

"Lucrative." Her eyes widened with sarcasm. "But I think I'll pass."

"So what *will* you do?" Laura tried again as Mandy layered several slices of cheese and turkey onto her sandwich.

"Probably head down to Spero Heights," she said, grunting as she popped open the pickle jar. "It's a pretty nice little town, and there are hardly any humans. Plus, most of the girls I used to work with are thinking about staying there after they get out of rehab."

It was a good, safe plan, but my heart dropped at the thought of her leaving. Even more so than the thought of

Laura going back to Hollywood. "But you worked so hard, reading that K9 manual from cover to cover."

"Twice," she added with a pointed look. "But if you're not joining Blood Vice, then I sure as hell ain't."

"What?" My hand squeezed the blood bag a little too tightly. A stream of tacky red squirted out onto my white tank top.

"There's an idea," Laura said, folding her arms and raising both eyebrows at me.

"That's the only other place my recent training would be useful," Mandy went on in spite of my horrified expression. "But I don't like bloodsuckers enough to deal with them directly."

"But…I thought you didn't want anything to do with House Lilith." I ignored the blood on my shirt and resumed anxiously sucking on the bag in my hand.

Mandy shrugged. "That was before they helped bring down the Scarlett Inn. All I knew about them before that were rumors being spread by the scum of the underworld."

So it was either say goodbye to both Laura *and* Mandy and begin a job I would undoubtedly loathe, or attempt to work with the likes of Roman Knight. If that wasn't a rock and a hard place, I didn't know what was.

Something low in my stomach clenched anytime I thought of the half-sired agent who'd taken over the case that had started this whole undead mess I was in. After feasting on his blood, I felt irrationally attracted to him. Irrationally, because other than his blood, I couldn't stand the guy. He was rude and broody, and getting the tiniest sliver of information out of him felt like a hostage negotiation.

"So, what's it going to be?" Mandy asked, flattening her tower of a sandwich with the heel of her hand. She lifted it to her lips and gave me a quizzical frown before cramming a corner of the monstrosity into her mouth.

The alarm on my wristwatch buzzed, alerting me that sunrise was fifteen minutes off. *Saved by the bell.* I held my hand up and tapped the face of the watch. "Darkness calls. We'll have to finish this conversation later."

# Chapter Three

I was dreaming again. It seemed like such a little thing, but I cherished it. Even though the dreams were bizarre and more lucid than I remembered from when I was alive. Then there was the awkward fact that they were all in shades of red. Win some, lose some, I guess.

The dreams also featured more unfamiliar faces than I was used to. A lot of young men and women. Occasionally, I spotted Vin. And Roman. I had a growing sense of unease about what it all meant. I'd never been one to put much stock in decoding dreams, but I'd also never been one to believe in things like vampires and werewolves. It didn't get more *woke* than this.

Tonight I dreamed of Vin, of the two of us attending our ten-year class reunion together—something I absolutely refused to do, no matter how much he pestered me about it. In the dream, when everyone went to lift their drinks for a toast, Vin handed me a blood bag as if it were no big deal, much to my horror—and everyone else present. It was so much worse than the naked-in-front-of-the-whole-department nightmares I'd endured as a human.

Dr. Vincent Hart, my high school crush and the local morgue doctor, had become my supplier through a half-bogus research project that he'd convinced some local college students to donate blood to. The legitimate half of his research stemmed from the bit of blood I let him draw from me—that I explicitly explained could not be shared with anyone else, for any reason, whatsoever.

If House Lilith found out I was willingly giving my blood to a human doctor for research, I would be deader than dead. Vin knew this, and he'd promised the results would stay between us. He claimed he was only using the research to feed his curiosity—and mine.

Roman hadn't been very forthcoming with the how-to-be-a-vampire questions I'd asked during our tense stakeout. It was more than a little annoying that he was only half-sired and hoarded these vital facts as if I should have to earn them. The prick. So I let Vin take my blood and discover what he could about my mysterious new condition. Which so far, wasn't much.

In addition to being my supplier, Vin was also my boyfriend now. Sort of. We went out on dates anyway. Never anywhere for dinner, obviously. But to movies and art galleries. On one of the rare weekend nights I'd had off, he'd taken me to the City Museum. It stayed open until midnight on Saturdays and Sundays. We were even planning to attend a late Cardinals game soon.

I hadn't bitten Vin since the first time when he almost passed out on me. The experience had left a bad taste in my mouth—no pun intended—though it hadn't stopped Vin from offering his throat every chance he got. He seemed desperate to give it another go, and for the life—er, death— of me, I couldn't figure out why. We hadn't slept together yet either, which seemed even weirder to me than drinking his blood.

Vin was less persistent in that regard, though I could tell he wanted me. My reservations had more to do with controlling my bloodlust than not wanting him back. He was a wantable enough guy, in a nerdy, Clark Kent sort of way. He stayed in shape, and he practiced good hygiene. He opened doors and told me I was beautiful. And when he wrapped his arms around my waist and kissed me goodnight, I melted against him like butter on a biscuit.

I hadn't been so sure it would turn out this well, but Vin surprised me more and more every day. It was the sort of relationship any normal girl would swoon over. But therein lay the problem. Normal wasn't exactly in my repertoire these days.

I woke Sunday night to Laura sitting on the edge of my bed, a glass of murky cow blood grasped in her hand. My nose crinkled at the smell of the viscous fluid.

"You're out of the bagged stuff," she said, handing me the drink. I accepted it and took a reluctant swallow, cringing as if it were straight vodka. It burned all the way down.

"What's with the room service?" I asked. Laura didn't usually offer me blood unless she had something to say that she was pretty sure I didn't want to hear. She'd also curled her hair and was wearing a low-cut blouse with a massive push-up bra, creating the sort of cleavage that refused to be ignored.

She waited for me to choke down another drink before taking a deep breath. "Shooting for season nine of *Henry's Courtroom* begins in two weeks, and I've decided to return to the show."

I eyeballed her overflowing *assets* and made a face. "I take it you've already sealed the deal via video chat?"

Laura shimmied her shoulders and gave me a devilish grin. "I got an extra twenty thou per episode."

I set the Bloody Betsy down on my night table and buried my face in my pillow with a groan. "Please, just tell me you didn't take him back."

"I didn't, but I am going to stay in our—*his*—beach condo until I find a new place." Her eyes slid sideways, giving her intentions away. She expected him to woo her and talk her out of buying her own house. I could see it all over her face, but I bit my tongue. I couldn't figure out how to live my own life. What business did I have telling her how to live hers?

"Two weeks, huh?" I lifted my head and squinted at her. "Guess I'd better get some applications in so you can tackle any daytime interviews I might get stuck with."

Laura gave me a patronizing look. "Or you could take the one job you're actually qualified for, which would totally work around your little daylight handicap."

I narrowed my eyes at her, but she held my gaze. Laura had used my career in law enforcement as a reason to run off to California ten years ago. She'd insisted I was going to get myself killed just like our mother had, and she'd be damned if she would stick around to watch it happen. Now, she was encouraging me to take an even more dangerous law enforcement job with the same goal. The irony seemed lost on her, but maybe the fact that I was already dead took the edge off her fear.

I had to wonder if she wasn't also pushing me toward Blood Vice out of guilt. It was a bad idea—but no worse than her going back to the creep who had pigeonholed her career. If she could convince me to do this, then maybe she wouldn't feel so duped or guilty for her own decision.

Laura blinked, ending our staring match, and grabbed my hand off the bedspread. "You're going to have to start taking better care of your nails. I'm growing mine out for the show." On that note, she stood and left my bedroom so I could sulk in peace.

Our conversation from the previous night came back to me, and I thought of Mandy and her plan to move to Spero Heights. My stomach cramped. I wanted to blame it on the cow blood, but who was I kidding? I was going to miss the girl. A lot.

There was another option—one I'd only briefly considered. I could follow her and see if the little town of horrors had any job openings. But I couldn't bear the thought of selling my mother's house, and I didn't like the idea of moving into a new community when I was so attached to this one. It was too much, too soon. And then there was Vin to consider—and the steady supply of free blood.

Laura's head popped back inside my bedroom. "I'm taking Mandy out for dinner so you can have some privacy with *Dr. Love*. We'll be back in an hour or two." She rolled her eyes before disappearing again.

I glanced up at the clock on my night table. The glowing red numbers reflected off the glass of blood. 8:00 P.M. Vin would be here soon to restock my refrigerator.

I threw the covers back and headed for the shower. Maybe a little necking—above the skin only—would help take my mind off things. I tended to do my best thinking when I wasn't thinking at all. Of course, that's when I tended to screw things up beyond repair. Like getting myself killed. Like getting my partner killed—

*"He was a grown man who made his own choices. Just like your mother was a grown woman who made hers."* That's what Dr. Townsend, the department shrink, had told Laura when she went to my last therapy session. *"They knew that was the price of their service. Something they might one day have to pay. Your service could one day cost you this, too."*

No kidding. It was a little late for that particular speech. Though, I think it gave Laura a new measure of respect for the badge. Just in time for me to give it up.

I ran the latest version of my resignation speech through my head as I washed my hair and shaved my legs. I had quite the collection of scenarios that I'd dreamt up in between my nineteenth-century London fantasies. There was the one where I clocked Langford for making one too many sexist *jokes* at my expense. The one where I seduced him and lured him into the break room before bleeding him dry. The one where I quit in front of Mathis, my former captain, just so I could watch Langford chew off his own tongue trying to keep from saying anything off color—or, even better, the one where he didn't hold his tongue, and Mathis clocked him for me.

I smirked as I fingered the shampoo out of my eyes. While all of those scenes sounded like fun, they were more likely to go down in one of Laura's soap operas. The reality would probably be far less theatrical. I'd make up some mundane, human excuse for my departure, and that would be that.

Langford would probably make one last jab at me, and I'd fake laugh along because that seemed to shut him up the fastest. A passerby was more likely to ask what was so funny than what I was so upset about, and Langford couldn't have anyone else hearing what a brazen asshat he was.

I hissed as I nicked my knee with the razor and then turned into the spray of the showerhead to wash the shaving cream out of the way so I could inspect the damage. The cut hardly bled at all, sealing itself shut and vanishing before my eyes. Being a vampire wasn't *all* bad. I still sported a burn on my shoulder from a little daylight mishap shortly after my resurrection, but the three lines had faded to a dull, pinkish brown. I could live with that.

Immortality seemed like it should have been a nice perk, too. I couldn't deny that the thought of Laura discovering a gray hair before I did brought a smile to my lips, but it didn't last long when I realized that also meant she would eventually grow old and die. While I stayed exactly the same. Which brought up another issue. Eventually, I *would* have to leave St. Louis. If for nothing more than to keep the fact that I didn't age hidden. I planned on holding off as long as possible.

I finished my shower and slipped into a pair of jean shorts and a tank top before towel drying my hair. Then I brushed my teeth. With foamy paste dripping from my chin, I made a face in the mirror, snapping my fangs out to give them a quick brush, too.

My mutated eye teeth were becoming easier to control. It was awkward at first, trying to make use of muscles that I hadn't known existed—or that maybe hadn't existed in my human body. But now that I knew about them, it felt wrong not to build them up like any other muscle group. I sucked my fangs in and popped them out a few more times in a series of warmup exercises I'd invented for myself. If I ever did integrate into the vamp community, maybe this would prove useful. *Jenna Skye: Fang Coach of the Damned.*

The doorbell rang as I rinsed my mouth. I spat in the sink and hurried out of the bathroom. The Bloody Betsy Laura had made for me sat forgotten on my night table. I couldn't bring myself to finish it, not with Vin waiting on my porch with a cooler full of co-ed nectar.

"Special delivery," he called out as I opened the door. I tried to swallow my need long enough to give him an appreciative smile. We didn't have big plans to go anywhere tonight, but he looked good enough to eat, nonetheless.

Under the glow of the porch light, I took in his tan legs, stretching out from beneath khaki shorts. The sleeves of his pale blue dress shirt were rolled up to the elbows, and the top few buttons had been left undone, exposing a delicious triangle of his smooth chest. Natural, tawny highlights streaked through his dark hair, and a touch of pink lit his cheeks and nose as if he'd stayed out in the sun just a *little* too long. I could smell it on his skin, and it made me weak in the knees.

I slipped a finger in between the buttons of his shirt and tugged him toward me. "Come here," I said, the hoarse edge of my voice painting a grin on his lips.

Vin pushed the cooler under one arm and wrapped his other around my waist, connecting our hips as our mouths met. He moaned softly as our kiss deepened, and I echoed him. It was a blissful song that grew more desperate each time we did this. His tongue flicked out and skirted my top lip before venturing in further, searching for the tips of my fangs. It took all my effort to keep them tucked in.

When I broke away to catch my breath, I dipped my face under his chin and lay a quick kiss to the throbbing pulse point in his throat, enjoying the way he shuddered against my mouth. Vin moaned again, more in surprise, and then pressed a kiss to my temple.

"I was going to ask if you missed me," he said, leaning back to flash me a cocky grin. "But I think you've already answered that question."

I lifted an eyebrow as I wedged the cooler out from under his arm and headed for the kitchen. "I think the real question is whether or not *you* missed *me*," I said. "Especially with all the sun-kissed babes I'm sure you've encountered this summer." I gave his bronze skin a once-over.

"Compared to my queen of the night?" He lifted his chin and shook his head in a comically haughty gesture as he followed me. "Mortal peasants."

"Yeah." I huffed. "Mortal peasants who don't have to fear killing their boyfriends if they get too amorous."

"If you'd just let me tie you up—"

"Yes," I snapped. "That's exactly how I picture our first time. *So* romantic."

Vin sighed and propped an elbow on the kitchen counter. We'd had this conversation more than once. It was a dead horse I couldn't seem to stop beating. Remorse tangled up my insides as I looked away from him and squatted down in front of the refrigerator.

I positioned the cooler between my knees and popped open the lid. Inside, two dozen bags of blood had been lined up in three rows of eight each. It was enough for a full week if I rationed out three to four bags a day, but I could make it last for almost two weeks if I supplemented with cow blood and didn't mind being irritable as hell the whole time.

I opened the refrigerator and stuffed the bags inside the shelves that lined the door, all except for one. I bit into it and took a long drink before turning around to face Vin. He watched me with pouty lips. Instead of diving back into our familiar rhetoric, I decided to give him a glimpse of the harder stuff I was dealing with.

"Laura's leaving for L.A. in two weeks."

Vin's eyes bulged. He stared at me a moment as if trying to decide whether or not I was joking. Then he cleared his throat and stood up taller, pulling his arm off the counter. "What does that mean for you?"

I shrugged one shoulder and gave him a pained smile. "I'm not sure yet."

His eyebrows knit together, and I knew exactly what he wanted to ask next. *What does this mean for us?*

I didn't have an answer for that either. His eyes slid away from mine, and I took the opportunity to finish off the bag of blood in my hand. The plastic end curled up like an oversized ice pop sleeve. I threw it away in the trashcan under the sink and then led Vin back outside to the front porch.

"It's such a beautiful night," I said at the worried frown he shot me. From his twitchy panic, I could tell he'd thought I was going to dismiss him for the night. The idea stoked the flames of guilt deep in my gut.

I wasn't just using Vin for his access to free blood. And I wasn't keeping him around simply because he was one of the few people who knew my darkest truth. At least, that's what I kept telling myself. When he took my hand, and my heart fluttered, I could almost believe that, too.

Outside, lazy fireflies floated above the overgrown lawn and crickets chirped. The moon hadn't risen yet, letting the bright stars have full command of the sky.

Vin sat down on the edge of the porch, his long legs extending over the few steps that led to the sidewalk. He pulled me down to sit sideways on his lap. He wrapped one arm around the back of my hips, and the other he lay over the tops of my thighs, his fingers curling around my leg and dragging me closer to him.

"Is there anything I can do to help?" he asked, kissing my shoulder. "I could write a letter of recommendation. Or proofread your résumé." He paused to nip at the strap of my tank top. "Or you could just move in with me—"

"Vin." I leaned away and scoffed at what I'd assumed was a joke.

"What?" He gave me an innocent frown. "I make more than enough money for both of us, and we spend all of our free time together anyway…"

I tried to pull myself out of his lap, but he pinned me in place with his arms. "We are *not* moving in together. It's far too soon to even think about that."

"Why?" Vin gave me a squeeze and kissed my shoulder again, trying to mollify my anxiety. "We're both adults. Who's going to stop us?"

"Vin, this is a bad idea—"

He cut me off with a kiss. When he pulled away, his nose grazed mine. "Just think about it," he whispered, muffling my reply with his lips again.

I relented and wrapped my arms around his neck. Kissing, I could do. Especially if it kept him from saying anything else that made me want to run screaming down the road.

Vin's hand slipped between my legs. His fingers played with the frayed ends of my jean shorts and sent goosebumps over my balmy skin. My pulse hitched. I could hear it thrumming against my temples. After the fresh blood, it almost sounded human, rising and falling in time with the crickets' song. But the blood hadn't been enough to placate the ever-present hunger that afflicted me. I feared it might never be enough. This close to Vin's warm, sun-soaked body, there was no amount of blood that could keep me from wanting to sink my teeth into him.

I felt my fangs ache with the need for release and tried to push the feeling to the back of my mind, focusing on Vin's fingertips rubbing soft circles on my back, on the blissful ache building low in my stomach. But every strong emotion seemed to tap into that hunger. I couldn't separate it or shut it off.

Vin jerked beneath me suddenly. I gasped and pulled away, one hand instantly going to my mouth where his hot blood spilled over my bottom lip. He snatched my wrist before I could wipe it away.

"It's okay," he whispered, shushing me as I tried to apologize. More blood coated his lips. "Baby steps," he said. "Maybe that's just what we need." He leaned in slowly, his eyes never leaving mine. He stopped a hairbreadth away from my mouth.

My fangs had retracted, but the warm tang of his blood sent a shiver through me. It was nothing like the bagged variety, which was still a far cry better than the cow blood. There was a world of difference between them all. Like going from dehydrated astronaut food to prime rib.

My tongue crept out slowly, lapping the blood from my bottom lip first. I closed my eyes with a heavy breath and savored every drop. Then I devoured Vin's mouth, licked it clean, searching for the source so I could probe it for more. His breath labored against mine, and when he jolted beneath me again, I was afraid I'd gone too far.

"Good evening," a rough, annoyed voice said from the lawn at my back.

If my fangs could have retracted up into my eye sockets, they probably would have. I ran my tongue over my lips one more time, hoping to clean any traces of blood from them, and then turned to face Roman.

Despite the muggy heat, he was wearing black pants and

a turtleneck that hugged his wide chest and massive shoulders. It was very urban ninja with a touch of commando, but his fluff of white hair ruined the effect. Even when he chose to cover his 'do with a stocking cap, those icy blue eyes made him stand out like a peacock in a dessert.

"What do you want?" I said, not bothering to hide my irritation. Vin tensed, and his arms tightened around my waist. Roman ignored him, reserving his broody scowl just for me.

"You haven't been returning my calls."

# Chapter Four

$V$in sat up taller and pushed his chest out so abruptly that, if not for his vice-like grip on my legs, I would have fallen right out of his lap.

"I remember you," he said to Roman, flashing a nervous smile. "You're the FBI agent who took over Jenna's case. Knight, wasn't it?"

Roman acknowledged him long enough to glare. "Special Agent Roman Knight. Have we met?"

Vin sniffed, the sound coming out more startled than offended. "Dr. Vincent Hart, St. Louis County Medical Examiner."

I gave Roman a dirty look, knowing full well he remembered meeting Vin at the morgue. Roman had called him my *beau*. It was an old-timey word that served to remind me he was much older than he appeared.

Being half-sired had its perks, and, truth be told, I would have preferred it to being a vampire. Roman could enjoy real food and sunlight, yet still cash in on the anti-aging and extra strength benefits of being a vamp. It wasn't fair. It made his brooding even more intolerable. What the hell did he have to be so grumpy about all the time?

"What do you want?" I repeated, the words grating through my clenched teeth. I uncoiled my arms from around

Vin's neck but didn't move from my perch on his lap.

"I have a case I need to discuss with you. In private," he added with a nod at the house as if he expected me to invite him inside.

Vin cleared his throat and loosened his grip on me, moving to stand. I resisted, grunting as he pulled me up, too.

"Sounds like it could be important," he said when I huffed at him. "I'll be up late. Give me a call when you're free." He brushed my hair over my shoulder and kissed my cheek. Then he gave Roman a curt nod before cautiously edging past him and moving toward his lime-green Volkswagen Beetle parked on the street. Roman waited for the car to rattle to life and pull away before turning his full attention back to me.

"Next time you feel like biting your friend, take it indoors." His voice was low and threatening, like an officer lecturing a drunk driver. It sent my temper into overdrive.

"There was no one out here to see us—except for you. Pervert." I snorted and put my hands on my hips. "Whatever it is you want from me, the answer is no. I'm not interested in chasing down bad guys just to let them run off into the night. My bad guys go behind bars." I almost choked on the words as I remembered the vampire I'd helped escape the night before.

"Those were special circumstances." Roman pressed his

lips together and raised an eyebrow at me. "Most of my bad guys are sleeping with the fishes."

All the air left my lungs. I had to swallow a few times to get my throat to work again. "That sounds like even more reason to avoid working with you."

Roman nodded as if he could appreciate my resistance. "I wouldn't be here if this didn't concern you directly," he admitted. The lump returned to my throat. It made sense. He hadn't seemed to enjoy working with me either.

My hands slipped off my hips, and I sighed. "Fine." I pushed the front door open and waited for him to climb the porch steps before entering ahead of him. "Make it quick. Laura and Mandy will be back soon."

Roman followed me into the kitchen, taking in the dove-gray walls, the white cabinets, and the new quartz countertop. Laura and I had bonded over the remodeling project, inspired by the giant hole Mandy had created in the wall the night I discovered her squatting in my house. Which also happened to be the same night Laura had arrived, like my very own bizarre little intervention team. Without the two of them, I wouldn't have survived the summer.

Roman took in the new fixtures with a blank expression, then he glanced at the window over the sink and the sliding glass door behind the dining room table. Probably checking for assassins or spies. Or a speedy exit should I try to bite him, too. He didn't exactly have a high opinion of me.

The last time Roman had been in my home, he'd pointed a rifle in my face. To be fair, he had just caught me snacking on a gangbanger in East St. Louis. But in my defense, the guy had tried to carjack me. And I'd been hungry. The memory made the gums around my fangs throb.

I opened the refrigerator and pulled out a bag of blood. Then I caught sight of Roman's pinched frown and blushed. "Do you want something to drink?"

"No."

"I have soda and Gatorade in here, too," I said, opening the door wider for him to see.

"I'm good." His eyes took in the rows of bagged blood. "I hope your friend isn't doing anything illegal to get his hands on that much product for you."

My nostrils flared at the baited accusation. "I'm pretty sure you'd know before I did if my *friend* were ransacking blood banks around the city."

"It's my job to ask these kinds of questions."

"That's funny. I didn't hear a question," I said, propping a fist on my hip. "Just a nasty, speculative remark."

Roman made a frustrated noise and shook his head. "You should set up a proper blood harem. It's the responsible thing to do. You'd require half as much if you drank exclusively from the source, and your strength would increase faster, too."

I slapped the bag of blood down on the counter and glared at him. "You say that like I should know better. How the hell would I know *any* of this? You made it sound like mingling with other vampires would bring up too many questions about my sire, and it's not like I can waltz into a library and ask where their nonfiction vampire section is!"

Roman grimaced, and I realized that my voice had escalated into a shout. I'd also inched across the kitchen until I was standing right in front of him, looking up into those frosty blue eyes, inhaling his earthy body heat. The knot of anger in my gut loosened. *Damn pheromones.* My chest heaved as I took a careful step back and reached for the blood bag, ready to devour it.

"I'm sorry," Roman said, almost causing me to choke on my first mouthful of blood.

"What?" I rasped.

"You're right. I should have been more helpful. I counted on the mutt having enough experience with vampires to get you through the transition, but I should have known better." *Mutt.* He was talking about Mandy, and however politically correct the term might be, I didn't like it. But I let it go this time because he was actually apologizing. I couldn't spoil that.

"Go on." I watched him with expectant eyes as I sucked on the bag of blood.

Roman grinned. It was slight, and I almost missed it. Just a gentle lift of one side of his mouth. "If you help me, I'll divulge everything I know about being a vampire."

I eased around the counter and onto a barstool. "Tell me about this case."

Roman glanced at the empty seat beside me but chose to stand on the opposite side of the counter instead, putting a safe stretch of distance and an obstacle between us. He folded his hands behind his back, assuming a military stance as if this were a formal debriefing.

"For the past six weeks, someone has been targeting new vamplings in St. Louis. Those without an active sire are especially vulnerable, their casualties roughly double those with local sires."

"Wait a minute." I held up a hand to stop him. "There are other vampires in the city like me?"

"Maybe not quite as new as you are—"

"But without a sire?"

Roman dipped his head in a quick nod. "Their sires are either dead or inactive, loosing their novice scions on the world long before they're ready."

"Oh, so you actually care what happens to these particular vamplings?" I said, my lips sagging into a condemning scowl.

"I apologized, didn't I?" Roman's eyes met mine briefly before he continued. "The similarities in the deaths are striking enough to categorize this as the work of a serial killer. That they are only going after the youngest and weakest means we could potentially be looking at a human predator. Their tendency to move bodies around during the day also supports this theory, though they could be working with a half-sired accomplice."

"Like you?" I injected. He scowled as if he'd forgotten I'd pried that detail out of him already. My job made me good at asking questions, too. "How many victims are we talking about here?"

Roman locked eyes with me again. "As of last night, six confirmed dead—though a dozen more have been reported missing."

My hands clenched the empty blood bag, and I took a slow breath. "And you think I can help how, exactly?"

Roman gave me an apprehensive look, and I knew the answer before he said it. "We could really use a vampling with police training who knows what they're doing—"

"To play bait," I finished, shaking my head. "Uh-uh. No way. You don't want my help. You want a carrot you can dangle in front of a psychopath you've been chasing in circles for the last six weeks. Do you really think I'm that stupid?" I bit my tongue before I started shouting again.

"You'd be paid. Well." He pulled a hand out from behind his back and ran it through his hair. "And I meant what I said before about telling you everything I know."

"That's assuming I survive." I scrunched up my nose at him. "That's assuming you don't intentionally let me die so you don't have to follow through."

The corners of his mouth twisted down in offense. "Is that really what you think of me? I spilled my blood for you. I don't do that for just anyone."

"Why *did* you do it?" I asked, my breath tightening at the memory. The event played out in my mind whenever I so much as thought his name. I could recall the rich flavor of his blood as if it had never left my tongue, and it stirred a moan at the back of my throat that I had to swallow, lest I humiliate myself. It was obscene, the amount of time I spent reliving those few moments over and over.

"You were my responsibility that night," Roman said. His voice was tight and uneven as if he, too, struggled with the memory of it. "You were only there because I asked for your help."

"Because you blackmailed me into helping." I leaned back in my barstool and folded my arms.

Roman nodded. "Even more reason for me to make sure you didn't die. I'm not a monster. I didn't let anything happen to you then, and I won't now."

"But you're more than happy to let me grope around in the dark to figure out this whole vampire thing on my own."

Yeah, that was a sore spot I wouldn't be getting over anytime soon.

Roman's jaw flexed, and I could tell I was starting to get under his skin. He'd been trying so hard there for a minute, too.

"We didn't exactly part on civil terms," he said, giving me a pointed stare. "And maybe if you'd returned my calls, you wouldn't have had to do so much *groping* in the dark. It's difficult to impart information when someone's ignoring you."

I rolled my eyes. "Sure, that's why you called. I haven't known you for very long, but from what I've seen, sharing information isn't exactly a skill you've mastered."

"I've spent half a century learning the ins and outs of this world, and you think I should just recite those details to you like a breathing encyclopedia?" he snapped. "What is it you want to know so badly anyway?"

"Everything!" I leaned over the counter and glared at him. "The day you die and rise as one of the undead, you'll be fully prepared. I didn't even know that vampires *existed* until after I'd been one for a full day. How is that fair?"

Roman's face flushed. He took a shuddering breath before stepping in closer to the counter, narrowing the gap between us even more. "Fair? I've served for fifty years on Blood Vice, and I'll serve fifty more as a half-sired agent before I earn the privilege of becoming a vampire. Something you accomplished with one foolish mistake as a green detective."

I recoiled from him as if I'd been slapped. "You think I should have stayed dead?" His mouth opened, but I went on before he could deny it. "Most days, I wish I had, and that my partner had been the one to survive." I thought of Will and his family who still mourned him.

"That's not what I meant." Roman gripped the edge of the counter and looked down, hiding his face from me. My raw honesty had surprised him, and now he was uncomfortable. I was over-sharing, but I didn't care as long as my point was made.

"I didn't sign up for this. And if I was so shitty at my job, I don't see why you're asking for my help." I pressed my palms into the countertop and tried to breathe through my nose. Tears burned at the corners of my eyes, but I begged them to wait. "I think you should leave now."

Roman blinked at me as if he only just realized how much his words had stung. Then he blew out a half-hearted sigh and shook his head, though it looked as if maybe it was more at him than me. "You can't work for the human police forever. I'm amazed you lasted as long as you have."

"Amazed that I haven't made any more foolish mistakes or gotten anyone else killed?" The red spilling across my vision throbbed. "Get out of my house."

"Right." He tapped his fist on the edge of the counter, ignoring the expanding fog of wrath I was suffocating in. "You have my number. When you decide you're ready for those answers, all you have to do is call." He turned and headed for the living room.

"Maybe I'll hunt down a vampire and ask them my questions instead."

Roman paused and looked over his shoulder at me. "And maybe you'll find our serial killer first and not have backup. Don't be stupid, Jenna. If you want to meet another vampire, I can introduce you to my partner."

I snorted. "Are you jealous of your partner, too? Or did he earn his undead status the hard way like you did?"

"*She* was made a vampire a century before we met."

"She?" I thought of the dark-haired woman I'd seen in his SUV at the warehouse and again in the barn after he stopped me from taking out Scarlett. Roman sighed and made an awkward noise in the back of his throat. He really wasn't good at this sharing business.

"She's heading up this case. You'll meet her if you agree to help."

"I'll think about it." I rolled the empty blood bag between my hands and tried to keep a neutral expression until Roman turned and headed back through the living room. I waited until I heard the front door close behind him before I let out the breath I'd been holding.

Answers sounded nice. Playing bait for a serial killer, not so much. Especially when that murderer had a taste for vampires. And not *bad* vampires. Just the youngest and the weakest.

It was a worthy case, and I knew I should have agreed to help for that reason alone. But I wouldn't just be pretending to match the killer's type. I *was* his type. That changed things.

I had a lot to think about, but if this guy had already taken out six vampires and maybe a dozen more that just hadn't been found yet, there wasn't much time to lose. I could stay hidden inside my isolated, human-ish lifestyle and go undetected while innocent vamplings died around the city, or I could fang-up and make my debut in the underground society a memorable one.

My only reservation was Roman. He'd been so persistent about keeping me away from that world. It had felt like he was trying to protect me. After his heated confession tonight, I had to wonder if jealously wasn't partly to blame. Still, there had to be more to it than that. And he *had* promised to answer my questions. I had plenty.

Now, I knew exactly where to begin.

# Chapter Five

I listened to the most recent message Roman had left on my machine and programmed his number into my cell phone. He'd given me his card before, but I had been pretty sure I would never actually call him. So I'd thrown it away. I was still sitting at the kitchen counter, stewing over the idea of accepting his offer, when my phone rang. My teeth clenched as Ned Ricker's cell number lit up the screen.

"What's up, Ricker?" I answered, trying not to sound as annoyed as I felt. There was only one reason he'd call me on my night off.

"Skye," he groaned through the speaker. So dramatic. "I need you and Star to cover for me and Yogi tonight. We ate some bad Mexican food, and it's not agreeing with us." I heard his tongue click softly, and then Yogi joined in with a solemn howl.

"It can't be too bad if you keep going back for more." I slumped in my barstool and scowled even though he couldn't see me. "Langford would kick your ass if he knew how many table scraps you feed that poor beast."

"I know, I know," he said. "You're a lifesaver, Skye. I owe you big time. In fact, I'll work your Tuesday night shift so you can still have a two-day break."

"Damn right, you will." I hung up, not waiting for a thank

you or a goodbye. This was the third time Ricker had pulled this on me since I joined the K9 unit. I already knew that if I said no, he'd just call Langford and have him call me in anyway. As the low officer on the totem pole, it was expected of me. It didn't mean I had to like it.

The clock on my phone read 9:30 P.M. The night shift began in an hour. How convenient that Ricker had called when he did. He was probably still at the cantina he liked to frequent—probably still putting down margaritas and salsa like nobody's business. I had half a mind to stop in and confront him, but that would just end with me being labeled a party-pooping snitch. Not the way I wanted to be remembered after I left the force.

By the time I finished putting on my uniform and gear, Laura and Mandy had returned from having dinner. Mandy took one look at me and froze, her cheeks puffing up with outrage. "This is bullshit! You should've at least asked me first."

"Okay," I said dryly, fixing the button at the base of my throat. "Hey, Star, are you up for covering Yogi's shift?"

"No," she barked. "I am most definitely *not*. The season finale of Thrones is tonight."

"I'll just call the captain and let him know my dog said tonight isn't good for her. Her show's on, and she doesn't want to risk anyone dropping spoilers at work."

"Such bullshit." Mandy growled and stomped off toward the room she shared with Laura.

She'd be back and ready to go in a few minutes. Even though she was taking it out on me, Mandy knew I didn't have any choice in the matter. Unless I wanted to quit. Which I'd have to do soon enough anyway. The thought of giving up my badge bummed me, but quitting on Langford's team would make the chore more bearable.

"So," Laura said, giving me a knowing look as she leaned against the back of the sofa to remove her heels. "Am I giving Captain Mullet your notice in the morning?"

I smirked at the nickname, thanking my lucky stars that my flirty sister disliked Langford as much as I did. I fetched my duffle bag from the coat closet. "I guess you probably should if you're leaving in two weeks. I have some notes in here." I unzipped the bag and dug around until I found a bundle of paper-clipped index cards. I handed them to her.

Laura pouted out her bottom lip, and I noticed that she was wearing heavier makeup than usual. She was already prepping for her diva revival. I just hoped that she didn't sabotage my reputation in the process.

"Are you sure you don't want me to improvise something more…colorful?" she asked, thumbing through the cards.

"I just want a quiet exit," I said.

Laura paused on a card and flipped it around for me to

see. "Really? You want to use the starting-a-family bit on him?" She scoffed and held up the next card. "Failing health? You can't be serious. None of this shit applies to you. I could tell him that he's made your work life such a living hell that you've decided to give up law enforcement for good, and that would be more honest than any of this."

"*Quiet* exit," I repeated.

Laura huffed and folded her arms. "Fine."

"Plus, I might not be giving up law enforcement, after all."

Her manicured eyebrows lifted playfully. "I thought that was tall, blond, and broody we passed on the way in."

"Nothing's set in stone," I added under my breath as Mandy rounded the corner in wolf form.

Her dark fur would have been more intimidating, more wolf-like, if not for the way it faded to brown along her muzzle and over one eye. The softer color covered her legs and the tip of her tail, too. It was less noticeable in the darkness we often worked in.

Mandy's ears lay flat against her head, but she didn't growl at me as I knelt down to tighten the straps of her police vest. The material didn't have as much give as the last one she'd worn, and after shifting, it hung around her ribcage unevenly. She turned her head away, pointing her muzzle up in the air as I made the adjustments.

"I'm sorry," I said, resisting the urge to pet her. I'd learned that lesson once already. "I didn't want to go in tonight either. If it makes you feel any better, Laura is putting in our notice in the morning."

Mandy shot a sly glance up at Laura, who nodded in agreement. Then she yipped out a sound that I took as approval. I stood and grabbed the duffle bag.

"Guess you're not getting that three-day weekend, after all," I said to Laura with an apologetic smile.

She sighed and fanned herself with the notecards. "The things I do for love."

I still questioned whether her help was more an act of penance rather than love, but I didn't say so out loud. I was grateful either way, and it was nice having my sister back in my life, being able to share things with her again. She was the only family I had—unless I counted Mandy, who I claimed as my foster daughter anytime someone was nosy enough to ask.

My mother would have argued that it didn't count—but not to be cruel. She had been a foster kid herself, though her last foster family had thrown her out on her ass when they discovered she was pregnant with Laura and me. That was all she ever had to say about them. They were not a part of our lives, and they'd hardly been a part of Mom's life. Just the tail end of a string of families that was never *really* family. Not in the way that counted.

I wanted to be there for Mandy in a way that counted. I wanted to provide her with the home she'd never had growing up, even though she was technically an adult now. I didn't care. No one could stop me from offering, and no one could keep her from accepting. Our arrangement was unspoken, but she seemed to be on the same page.

I glanced down and gave her a small smile as we headed out the front door. "We have enough time to run by that pizza joint you like," I said. Her tail wagged, and she barked at me. In her wolfy state, her body responded instantly to the promise of food. Even though she'd just eaten with Laura, Mandy would be able to put down an entire pizza by herself. Shifting used up a lot of calories, which could be seen in her petite human form.

My smile stretched wider. "I hope that means I'm forgiven." When she grumbled, I added, "Besides, we're just running basic patrol around the city tonight. It's Sunday. What's the worst that could happen?"

I enjoyed the slow nights when it was just the two of us on patrol. Since we had to be so cautious about what we did, solo work was our safest bet. I didn't have to pretend to be human around Mandy, and she didn't have to pretend to be a dog around me. And I also didn't have to worry about a human partner seeing something they shouldn't.

If things got a little weird with a suspect, no one would believe them over an officer. Langford, no matter how much he enjoyed giving me hell, would call them crazy before I even had a chance to dream up an excuse for their bizarre claim. Not that he'd ever had to.

Mandy and I had been very careful. Her certifications were fabricated under the guise that the hard copies had been lost in a fire. That's how I explained my ability to "purchase" her for such a steep discount. That she was so excellently "trained" helped drive the lie home. Of course, we also had to be careful that she didn't appear too well-trained. It would have been easy to blow all the K9 records out of the water. In fact, it was harder trying not to break records.

Mandy had to be good enough to be accepted onto the unit without additional pre-training, but not so good that we found ourselves on House Lilith's radar. It was an awkward challenge after spending so many years striving for perfection and promotion, training to be considered average rather than exceptional. But we pulled it off, and of that, I was proud.

Mandy napped in the seat next to me, her muzzle propped on the lid of a pizza box. A smear of tomato sauce cut across her nose, and more clung to her whiskers. I eased on the brake as I rounded a corner so I wouldn't wake her.

Our routine was a fairly lazy one, but no lazier than Ricker and Yogi's.

Letting Mandy ride up front was technically against the rules, but the caged-off area behind us was meant for police dogs that couldn't understand things like someone trying to help their handler in the event of a crash. It was an accidental bite precaution. I only asked Mandy to ride back there for show when we I knew we were going to be seen by someone who would make a stink about it.

The speaker on the dash crackled, and Collins' voice summoned me. "K9-7, this is 215. I have one in custody and could use assistance at Page and Lakeland."

Mandy's ears twitched. Her head popped up as I replied to the call.

"K9-7, copy. En route."

I sighed, relieved that his suspect was already in custody. Sniffing a car for narcotics was easy for Mandy. Chasing someone down without chewing their limbs off was a bit more of a struggle. If her urge to kill prey was anything like my bloodlust, I pitied her.

Mandy and I didn't talk much about her biological condition. Everything she knew stemmed from a life she'd just barely survived, and I felt guilty any time I stirred those dark memories. That she was a sardonic teenager didn't make the conversations any more fun either.

As we turned west on Page Avenue, Mandy pressed her front paws into the floorboard and stretched. Then she slicked her long tongue over her muzzle a few times, washing away the evidence of her late-night snack.

"Probably just a quick car search," I said to her. I glanced at the clock on the dash and added, "Then we can take lunch." Her tail wagged at that, and she bared her teeth at me in a startling smile.

A few minutes later, we pulled off of Page and onto Lakeland. I spotted Collins' patrol car in a hotel parking lot sandwiched between a gas station and a Hooters. Two more hotels and an electrical supply company were nearby. Hooters' parking lot was empty. They closed at eleven on Sunday nights. The hotels weren't especially busy either, their lots holding only a handful of cars, most all of them haloed by the protective glow of security lights.

Collins' sergeant pulled in just as I did. I sucked in a tense breath and glanced at Mandy, trying to decide the best way to go about parking so that I could let her out of the car without giving away the fact that she'd been in the front seat with an empty pizza box.

With a little quick thinking, I pulled in on the opposite side of Collins' car, using it for cover. I hopped out and ushered Mandy through my open door. Then I opened and closed the back passenger door, hoping the sound was ruse enough. Mandy snorted at me, and I could have sworn I saw her golden eyes roll.

"Easy for you to scoff at the rules," I whispered as I knelt down to clip a leash on her collar. "You're not the one who'll get ripped a new asshole if we're busted."

When I walked Mandy around the cars, Collins and Sergeant Patz were waiting for us. Collins reclined against the side of his cruiser, arms casually folded across his chest. He was the epitome of comfortable confidence, and the sergeant's presence only made it more obvious. The older officer looked like an ostrich stretching its neck to gain more height. He was only an inch shorter than me, but Collins towered over him by a good four or five inches. He squared his shoulders and put his hands on his hips as I joined them.

Patz had been my commanding officer when I worked patrol, too. He was only in his fifties, but years of neglecting to wear sunblock had shriveled him up like a prune and filled his fair complexion with blotchy sunspots. It also led to a skin cancer scare that had cost him the top ridge of one ear. He spent more time on the late shifts now to reduce his sun exposure.

Patz was not my favorite person, but I'd gotten by without too much trouble from him when I worked patrol. He had the mindset of a much older generation, one that believed police work was meant for men, and that all women should be obedient housewives. We'd never warmed up to each other, but he was at least respectful enough to keep his outdated opinions to himself. For the most part. The scolding look he gave me as I stopped before him and Collins made me wonder if that had changed since I left patrol.

"Take a looksee," Collins said, nodding at the cruiser. He opened the back door and revealed the young suspect inside. The kid didn't look old enough to buy a pack of cigarettes. A cluster of zits dotted his forehead under the band of a backward Cardinals ball cap, and when he sneered at Collins, I could see the red, white, and blue rubber bands of his braces.

"I'm a minor," he shouted. "You can't arrest me. I know my rights!"

Patz snorted. "If you're a minor, then we'll turn you over to one of our juvenile corrections officers. Maybe you'll give *them* your name, because you're going to be in custody until we find out." The kid's eyes migrated away from the sergeant and landed on Mandy next.

"I told you we'd find the drugs," Collins said. "One way or another. Are you sure you don't want to make this easier on yourself and tell us where you ditched them?"

"I don't know what you're talking about. I don't do drugs." His throat bobbed, and he leaned back in his seat as Mandy crept closer, sniffing the air to catch his scent. Collins watched her, and when she eased back and sat on her haunches, he lifted an eyebrow at me. I nodded, letting him know we were good to go. He closed the cruiser door before filling us in on the rest of the story.

"The hotel just off Page called in suspicious activity, and I was closest to the scene," he said. "I arrived in time to witness the suspect engaged in a deal with another party."

"Another party?" Patz asked, placing his hands on either side of his belt buckle. His neck strained as he rocked up off his heels, leveling with me for a brief moment.

Collins nodded. "The dealer took off, but I called in a BOLO. This one wasn't fast enough. I imagine he's got a car around here somewhere, but since I can't even get a name out of him, I haven't had much luck."

"Hmm." Patz rubbed his chin. "I'll make a note for someone on day shift to check in with the surrounding businesses in the morning. Maybe they can locate some surveillance footage or at least narrow down the search through process of elimination." He turned to me next. "Are you waiting for a formal invitation to do your job, Skye?"

I stiffened and turned my attention to Collins, ignoring the barb. "Is there anything else you'd like to share before we begin?"

Collins gave me an apologetic smile before answering. "There've been a few hard drug busts around here recently, so you might want to keep close to Star so she doesn't accidentally ingest anything. The suspect cut through the hotels between here and Page." He pointed the way, and Mandy and I set off without sparing another look in Patz's direction.

The chip on the sergeant's shoulder had clearly grown since our last encounter. It was as if he'd taken my promotion to detective as a personal insult to his leadership. I wouldn't lie, I'd enjoyed working under Mathis more, however short-lived the job had been. But I didn't make the move out of spite for Patz. It was one I'd made with my mother in mind.

By the same token, I hadn't applied to the K9 unit wholly for Mandy's sake. It wasn't even just to protect my new secret or because I wasn't ready for another human partner so soon after losing Will. Mandy's life was every bit as valuable as a human's. I was doing this because my mother had. Because I wanted to wrap myself in her world as if that might somehow keep the reality that she was gone from suffocating me. That, more than anything, stabbed at my heart when I thought about my pending resignation.

Mandy's nose dipped to the ground a time or two as we hurried across the parking lot and around the backside of the hotel. My shoulders sagged once we were out of Patz's line of sight. His stiff posture was contagious, and I certainly didn't miss that constant feeling of being scrutinized and silently snubbed.

Mandy tugged me toward a thin line of trees that separated the hotel's parking lot from a secluded truck bay. White cinderblock walls peeked through the branches and tall grass. I ducked under the prickly arm of a pine tree and slid down an embankment, catching myself before I wiped out on the pavement below.

Security lights revealed a few dumpsters in between metal stairwells leading to the buildings' back exits. As Mandy led me forward, I tried to guess where the kid had stashed the drugs. Maybe behind one of the stairwells or dumpsters? Under the nest of brush in the far corner?

Mandy urged me farther along, into the truck bay behind the next building over. In her wolfy form, she couldn't explain to me what she was processing with her nose, but our path painted a fairly clear picture. The kid had circled the group of buildings, likely hoping to make his way back to a vehicle. My money was on the blue minivan I'd spied in the hotel parking lot closest to Hooters. It was probably registered to his mother.

We'd almost cleared the second truck bay when Mandy paused and glanced over her shoulder. A soft whimper wheezed through her flared nostrils as she eyed a knot of trees that bordered the drive leading out of the truck bay. A faded sign was erected in front of them, listing the buildings grouped together there, their otherwise unmarked lots all blending together.

Mandy took off again, stopping in front of the sign and poking her nose in a bush beside it. She pawed the cedar mulch, turning up the earth until the corner of a plastic baggy surfaced.

"That's good," I said, giving her leash a gentle tug. "Let the old curmudgeon do his part from here." I reached for the radio clipped to my uniform, but Mandy jerked the leash, almost pulling me off my feet. "Hey!"

She answered with a perturbed growl and dragged me around the other side of the thicket. Her dark fur and black police vest disappeared in the shadows of the trees, but she kept pulling me forward. I lifted my free arm up to shield my face from the low-hanging branches. The sticky pine needles grated against my skin and snagged my ponytail.

"What the hell, Mandy?" I hissed, and then the toe of my boot connected with something solid on the ground. A musty, metallic odor drifted up from the darkness pooling around my legs. It was both familiar and foreign, like a favorite perfume when it starts to go bad.

Mandy growled again as I grabbed the flashlight off my belt and clicked it on, eager to see what she'd found. The light bounced off the greenery pressing in all around me. I dropped the leash so I could free my other hand to push the limbs back away from the ground.

When I saw it, I choked back a scream.

The body had been stripped nude. Sickly, gray flesh glowed under the beam of my flashlight, picking out every cut and bruise on the slender, feminine form. Her wrists and ankles were raw, but whatever bindings she'd struggled against were now gone. I pushed more branches out of the way, searching for her face.

The urge to scream hit me again as I found the bloody stump of her neck. She'd been decapitated. Red washed over my vision, reacting to the adrenaline that shot through me, but her skin remained the palest of grays.

*Vampire.*

I reached for my radio again out of instinct. Mandy whined, and my finger froze over the call button. I wasn't thinking clearly. Panic had seeped into my bones, and I'd fallen back on my human training. It was no good right now.

My radio buzzed, and I jumped as Patz's voice crackled in my ear. "You plan on taking all night, Skye?"

"We're still on the trail," I answered, consciously lowering my voice an octave so I wouldn't sound alarmed. The lie wouldn't hold him off for long.

This dilemma wasn't one that could be fixed with a fog of pepper spray. I knew what I had to do. I'd just hoped I could avoid it a little longer.

I sighed and glanced down at Mandy's worried face as I

pulled my cell phone out of my pocket. Then I dialed Roman's number.

# Chapter Six

Yellow crime scene tape marked off the truck bay, and seven FBI vehicles—including Roman's unmarked SUV—were parked around the cluster of trees and bushes where I'd found the headless vampire. Blue and red lights flashed through windshields, but no sirens sounded, and the agents themselves were deathly silent as they worked. There were about a dozen of them, all in the same ninja-commando getup that Roman wore. They swarmed the area, pressing the perimeter out so far that no one who dared to get close enough would be able to see anything. Including me.

"Do you have any idea how much hot water you're in?" Collins asked. We stood in the back parking lot of the hotel, the closest we could get to the scene.

"I don't know what you're talking about." I was prepared to lie my ass off tonight—even to Collins, whose patience had worn thin with me lately. No need to put him in a bad position just because I was in one.

Collins glanced over his shoulder, back to where Patz sat in his cruiser, headlights shining through the sparse tree line. I couldn't see past his tinted windshield, not without my blood vision, but I imagined he was glaring at me in between squinting through the binoculars he kept stashed in his glovebox.

Collins had moved his cruiser around to the back of the hotel, too. A juvenile corrections officer was on the way to collect the kid in his back seat. Collins was a true friend, not leaving me alone to face the wrath of Patz by myself. It made lying to him that much harder, but even more necessary to protect his job. I would have hugged him if I weren't so worried about the sergeant taking it out on him afterward.

A faint rustling of leaves drew my attention back to the trees. Two agents were walking up the embankment on the other side. As they neared where we stood, Patz's car door opened and slammed shut behind me.

"I hope you know you're interfering with a local investigation," Patz shouted before they'd completed their ascent.

Roman stepped out of the shadows first, quickly joined by the dark-haired woman I'd seen him with before. I hadn't gotten a good look at her in the barn when Roman had stopped me from shooting Scarlett as she made her escape. My blood vision had put a haze over everything at the time, and I'd been too focused on how much I wanted to strangle Roman than how beautiful his partner was.

She stood a good four inches taller than me, nearly shoulder-to-shoulder with Roman. A long, black braid hung over the breast pocket of her tactical vest, obscuring an embroidered logo. Her milky skin contrasted strikingly with her features, despite the shadows of the parking lot. Deep red lips, dark brows, thick lashes, and the greenest eyes I'd ever seen. Those eyes settled on me, and a flash of uncertainty shot through her gaze before the neutral expression returned and her attention snapped onto Patz.

The sergeant stopped directly in front of them, his hands going to either side of his belt buckle. He rose up on his toes, but he still came up short and had to tilt his head back to look up into Roman's face.

"This was my crime scene first," he shouted. "I have an ongoing investigation, a suspect in custody, and a K9 officer tracking down drugs. You're interfering wi—"

"Special Agent Roman Knight," Roman interrupted, holding up the badge that hung from a chain around his neck. His partner did the same.

"Special Agent Vanessa Sorano." She inclined her head and blinked her sharp eyes at the sergeant. "We've shown you ours. Now, you show us yours."

Patz took a step back. He squinted at their badges even as he lifted his palms. "There's no need to get your panties in a twist, ma'am. I'm just doing my job." He knew he was stepping out of line. He might have talked a big game, but he didn't want to lose his job. Vanessa wasn't the type to tolerate his arrogance for one minute. I instantly respected that about her.

When Patz didn't reach for his badge or identify himself, Roman turned his questioning glance in my direction. I blinked at him, my eyes going wide. He expected me to confess to dialing his number, right in front of the sergeant. Patz had probably already guessed that this was my fault, but now he'd have all the proof he needed.

I huffed out a perturbed sigh. "Sergeant Brent Patz, 2nd Precinct." I nodded my head at Collins next. "Officer Max Collins, 2nd Precinct. Neither of them saw or know anything." That earned me a dirty look from both men.

"Good," Roman replied, some of the tension leaving his shoulders.

"You can have the drugs," Vanessa said, holding up the plastic bag of heroin. "We've even forwarded pictures of *your* scene to your superior, Captain Mathis."

Patz's mouth dropped open as he took the bag from her. He choked out a surprised sound. "But…but we didn't see it with our own eyes!"

Vanessa's impassive expression never changed. "You may direct all further questions about this matter to your superior, Captain Mathis. Now, if you'll excuse us, we must get back to work. The scene will be cleared within two minutes—if you'd like to check for any additional evidence regarding *your* investigation."

As she spoke, I glanced through the trees behind her.

Someone was already tearing down the crime scene tape. One agent scrubbed at a spot in the concrete with a deck brush while another poured a bucket of water over the suds, rinsing the area clean. Two of the vehicles pulled away as they finished up.

Roman and Vanessa turned and headed back through the trees without another word. Patz and Collins gawked after them, baffled and fuming. Then their gazes turned at the same time to stare at me.

"Whose fucking side are you on, Skye?" Patz shouted. "What the hell was that about?"

I looked to Collins to back me up, but his face was perfectly blank as if he, too, couldn't understand what had just happened.

"They're FBI." I shrugged. "I'm not going to go down with your dumb ass for interfering with a federal case."

Patz's face screwed up, and his chest expanded as he inhaled an enraged breath. "I'm calling this in to Langford. You might as well head back to his office."

"And what do you plan to tell him?" I folded my arms. "That your *panties are in a twist,* all because I cooperated with the FBI while you refused to even identify yourself?" I stalked off, not waiting for his reply. Mandy trotted along beside me. The fur down the exposed stretch of her hind end was raised. I tightened my grip on her leash as Patz screamed after me.

"Disrespectful insubordination! That's what I'll be telling your captain, young lady. Get your ass back to the station!"

"Fuck you," I grumbled over my shoulder without turning around.

"What the hell did you just say?" I heard the sound of Patz's boots on the pavement behind me.

I was more concerned about getting Mandy into the police car than I was about the sergeant engaging in a physical altercation with me. Patz might scream or wave around an indignant finger, but I didn't think he'd ever actually hit a woman. Mandy didn't know that, but she'd eat his face off either way.

I shouldn't have egged him on. I knew what a fragile ego he had, but my nerves were still shot from finding the body. And we were late taking lunch. My bloodlust cranked up my irritation and obliterated my tolerance for Patz's little-man syndrome.

I opened the back door of my cruiser and hustled Mandy inside, ignoring the low growl building in her throat. Her golden eyes were full of wrath. I closed the door just as Patz reached us.

"What the *hell* did you say to me?" he screamed in my face, spit shooting from his thin lips and trailing down his chin.

"Fuck. You," I repeated slowly, refusing to raise my

voice. When his chest bumped into mine, I narrowed my eyes at him. "Go ahead and put your hands on me. See if you still have a job tomorrow."

He drew back an inch, his fists clenching at his sides. "We'll see who's unemployed tomorrow, young lady."

I shrugged. "I guess so. Until then, I have a job to do, and you're standing in my way."

His grimace stretched deeper into the pits of his jowls, but he sidestepped out of my path as I opened the driver's side door of the cruiser.

"And to all a goodnight," I said, more to myself than to him.

Patz looked as if he wanted to throw himself on the ground and have a full-blown tantrum, but just then, an unmarked car turned into the parking lot. I guessed it was the juvenile officer coming to collect the kid from Collins. I didn't wait around to find out.

Patz was distracted long enough for me to start the cruiser and pull away from the scene. I watched his irate face fade into the distance through my rearview mirror. It brought a small smile to my lips.

I held the steering wheel with one hand and dug a blood bag out of the backpack looped behind the front passenger's seat. I was going to need the pick-me-up before facing Langford. If Patz had been bluffing about calling my captain, he'd certainly follow through now. Someone would be getting an earful, and since I hadn't hung around for it, Langford would be next in line.

*Did I regret my behavior?*

I tried to ask myself the question more honestly after I'd sucked down half of the blood bag.

*Nope.*

Someone needed to knock the jerk off his high horse. I was as good a candidate as any—maybe even better for the fact that I'd only have to suffer the consequences of my actions for another two weeks. Or less, if I couldn't keep my mouth shut with Langford either.

I grabbed another blood bag and prayed for endurance as I pulled out onto Page Avenue and headed back toward the station.

An anti-smoking poster adorned the back wall of Langford's office. The graphic was stylized like pop art, showcasing a revolver loaded with smoking cigarettes. The tiny text to the left of the graphic listed all the horrible things tobacco did to the body, but against the dotted, comic book background, the message was lost. It was about as effective as using a painting of a Porsche to encourage drivers not to go over the speed limit.

The poster had been there long before Langford came along, and I was sure that I wasn't the only one surprised that he'd left it up. His office reeked of cigarette smoke. The station was *Proudly Tobacco-Free* according to the sign on the front door. The county had even paid for several officers to have acupuncture treatments to relieve cravings and help them quit.

Langford refused the offer, denying he smoked as if we couldn't smell him coming from a mile away. Even as I sat waiting in his office, I detected his menthol aura as he lumbered down the hallway, closing in on our inevitable confrontation.

Mandy lay on the floor at my feet, pretending to doze. Her ears remained perked, and I could hear the steady thrum of her heartbeat. It was too hot outside to leave her in the cruiser, even in the dead of night, though I'd cautioned her not to react while Langford lectured me on respecting my superiors. It was better for everyone if I just took my lumps.

Since Patz had roused the captain early from bed, he was bound to be in a hostile mood. It probably wasn't ideal timing, but I decided to go ahead and put in my two-week notice myself, rather than risk Laura taking the opportunity to practice her soap opera drama.

My anxiety tinged everything in shades of pink, but I kept

my cool, lifting my hand to examine my nails once I sensed Langford's rotund presence in the doorway at my back. I'd let him run off at the mouth, but I was not the actor in the family. I would not be begging and pleading for mercy. I did not cower before anyone. It just wasn't how I was raised. The fact that I was a royal vampire scion now probably didn't help in the humility department either.

"Well," Langford said, louder than necessary as if he hoped to startle me. "What do you have to say for yourself?" He circled his desk and paused to yank up his pants before sitting down in the ratty leather chair he referred to as his throne. His salt-and-pepper mullet was no crown, and it was a struggle not to stare—or laugh—every time I looked at him. I was sure the hairstyle violated the department dress code, but no one had been brave enough to demand he cut it.

"Obstruction of justice is a felony." I lifted my chin.

"What are you talking about?"

"There was a deputy down south, just a few years back, who did hard time for lying to the FBI." I shook my head. "If Patz is okay taking that sort of gamble, that's his problem. Not mine."

Langford sighed and folded his hands over his desk as if he were disappointed by my answer. He tipped his chin down to give me a patronizing scowl, causing his thick neck to puddle under his jawline. He'd only been a pencil pusher for a couple of years, but he'd gone soft. Captain Mathis spent an hour in the gym every morning. *Man,* I missed working under someone who knew what they were doing, someone who was a professional.

"Insubordination with a superior officer is still a serious offense in this department—even for someone as pretty as you," Langford said, giving me a creepy wink. Then he clicked his tongue and fingered through a stack of papers on his desk. "But, pretty or not, I don't think Sergeant Patz is going to be satisfied unless I suspend you without pay for a week."

I shrugged. "How about you do us both a favor and make it two weeks?"

His hands froze on his desk, and his head jerked up. "Excuse me?"

"I was planning on putting in my two-week notice today."

Langford's cheeks flushed. His words garbled over his tongue a minute before he found his voice again. "You'll have to turn in an official resignation letter." He didn't even ask why I was leaving. Mathis would have cared enough to get to the heart of the matter.

"Already typed." I pulled my cell phone out of my pocket and found the document in my cloud drive. I attached it to a blank email and sent it on its way. "It should be in your inbox any second now."

Langford looked beside himself. This was clearly not how

he'd expected our conversation to go. His confusion and surprise quickly molded into resentment.

"I want your badge—" I slapped it on his desk before the sentence had left his mouth, along with my service weapon.

"Anything else?" I asked, standing.

"You'll have to return all the K9 training equipment in your possession, and your new cruiser."

"I'll have it all delivered to you by the end of the day." I patted my leg, rousing Mandy from her pretend nap.

"Star, too. In fact, you can leave her now." His mouth pinched into a cruel smile when he realized he'd finally gotten under my skin.

"I paid her purchase price. She's leaving with me," I said, forcing the words past the acid burning its way through my chest.

"Star is property of the St. Louis County Police Department," Langford insisted, giving me a jeering smile. "While we appreciate your generous donation, her most recent training has been at our expense, and we still have quite a few years left to earn back our investment."

Mandy's ears flattened, and a growl rumbled in the back of her throat. Langford's menacing gaze dropped to her, and he swallowed before rubbing a hand over the stubble on his chin.

"You can leave her in one of the kennels in back," he said

in a softer voice as if afraid his tone had agitated her. When she bared her teeth at him and took a step toward the desk, he wheezed out a startled breath.

"That's not happening." I gave him a sympathetic frown. "I'm afraid that Star won't listen to anyone else. Why do you think I got such a good deal on her?"

Langford scoffed, his laughter coming out as nothing more than a whisper. "I'm really sorry, Skye. That's just the way it is." He gave Mandy an anxious frown as her growl grew more intense. "Command her to stop that."

"I would," I said, holding one hand out in a helpless gesture, "but I've already resigned, so you're not actually my boss anymore. I guess that's just the way it is."

I turned and left his office, ignoring his shouts of protest. Mandy stayed glued to my side, her eyes darting around the quiet lobby as if she expected officers to jump out of the shadows and dogpile her any moment. Most of the day shift that stuck closer to the station wouldn't be in for another few hours. It was only four in the morning.

We made it to the side exit and out of the building without Langford giving chase. Maybe he wasn't as dumb as he looked. I opened my cruiser door and let Mandy into the front seat. She'd have to shift before we made it home, since I was pretty sure there would be a car waiting for us. Waiting to collect Star and stuff her in a kennel.

If they couldn't find her, that would be easy enough to avoid. I wasn't sure if that would be sufficient to keep them from arresting me for theft, though. Or from *attempting* to arrest me, anyway.

I would abso-fucking-lutely bite someone and drain them dry if they tried to put me in cuffs. The thought horrified me because I knew if I ever ended up in a cell, House Lilith would send someone to bust me out—if only so they could execute me themselves for being stupid enough to get caught by humans in the first place.

I fired up the cruiser and pulled out of the lot, merging into the meager, early-morning traffic. A crackling noise came from the passenger seat. Mandy's bones were reconfiguring themselves as she shifted. I diverted my gaze and focused on pushing the accelerator into the floorboard as we barreled down the street, putting distance between us and the station. If Langford misplaced his wits again, I wanted to be long gone before he even considered giving chase.

Laura was probably up by now. My stomach churned impatiently as I fumbled with my phone. I wasn't being a very responsible driver, but I didn't have a lot of time to fix this.

"Pick up, pick up, pick up," I chanted as Laura's phone rang.

"I'm awake," she grumbled.

"Put a uniform on," I snapped. "You're going to have

company soon. I just quit and took Mandy with me. Langford wasn't happy about it. Whoever they send, tell them she ran off as soon as you let her out of the car."

"Jesus, Jenna. I thought you said you wanted a quiet exit."

"I know!" I smacked the steering wheel. "Damn it. I know what I said. It didn't work out that way, all right?"

"But your cruiser isn't even here." Laura cleared her throat, and I heard the squeak of her mattress as she crawled out of bed.

"Tell them it's in the garage, that you'll be using it to return all of the training equipment by the end of the day like Langford requested. You've been nothing but compliant. Don't let them search the house without a warrant."

"What?" Laura's voice cracked. "Oh my God. I'm not going to get arrested, am I?"

"Don't be stupid." I tried to muster up a laugh, but my throat wouldn't work. "Just do what I said, and everything will be fine. I have to make another call."

I hung up before she decided to launch into a melodramatic monologue. Laura would be okay. I hoped. She was an actress, after all.

"She can totally pull this off," Mandy said, thrusting her hips up to button the cut-off jean shorts she'd fished out of the glovebox. "And I'll be a witness to the *escaped dog* story, but I'm using an alias. I don't want my name showing up in a human police report."

"Good. That's fine."

I fingered my phone again and held my breath as Roman's line rang. He owed me a favor after this morning. All of this was really his fault. At least, that was what I planned on telling him until he caved and helped me out of this mess.

"I'm at your house," he said by way of greeting. "You'll make it here five minutes before the unit being sent to arrest you."

"What? How?" I recalled the complex system that ate up the entire dash of his SUV. "You hacked the department's GPS system."

"Correction, I have security clearance to access any and all law enforcement GPS systems."

I smirked and cradled the phone between my ear and shoulder so I could use both hands to make a turn. Mandy grabbed the dash and wrestled her seatbelt on with her free hand, casting me a nervous frown as she listened in on my phone conversation with her wolfy hearing.

"And I guess you already know what I've stepped in, too," I said to Roman.

"Why else would I be waiting at your house?" he asked.

"So you're going to help me?"

"That depends." A stretch of silence followed that had me holding my breath, and then his smug voice tickled my ear. "Are you going to help me?"

I groaned, but it was the sound of defeat rather than refusal. "When you said *well paid…*"

Roman's laugh startled me, and I almost dropped my phone. It slid down the curve of my shoulder. When I pressed it back to my ear, he'd regained his composure.

"We'll talk numbers once I convince Officer Collins to leave without making an arrest."

My heart dropped. Langford had sent Collins. He could have sent Sergeant Patz and had a real catastrophe on his hands, but instead, he'd sent one of the few officers he knew I actually respected. I wondered if I should be worried about the sudden appearance of his brain. I guessed maybe he made captain for some other reason than his taste in vintage haircuts and gag-worthy charm.

"Jenna?" Roman was still on the line.

I didn't want to be arrested, but I didn't want Collins to lose his job either. I glanced across the car to where Mandy sat. I was the only stable adult she'd probably ever had in her life, which wasn't saying a lot. Still, I didn't want to let her down.

Accepting Roman's help was the only way any of this would end well.

"I'm in."

# Chapter Seven

Roman's timing was off, but I wasn't complaining. I figured Collins would drag his feet, giving me the extra minutes he probably thought I needed to say goodbye to Star.

Laura met me at the door in uniform, and then, after grabbing her hip and delivering an exasperated sigh, she retreated back to bed to resume her beauty sleep. Mandy followed her. Roman had insisted it wouldn't be necessary for her to make a statement. She looked skeptical, but she didn't argue.

Roman watched the two of them disappear inside with a pinched brow. "It's too bad you can't convince your sister to stay. I know you and the girl value your work with the police." It was an oddly heartfelt remark for him, but I guessed he was feeling less abrasive now that I'd agreed to help with his case.

"Maybe we can learn to value working with Blood Vice, too." I gave him a tight smile and closed the front door, joining him on the porch. His expression hardened as he turned back to me.

"This is just one job, Jenna. You'll be paid as an anonymous, undercover civilian."

"Sounds like a pretty good foot in the door to me," I said.

Roman took a deep breath. His brows drew together again, crinkling the skin between them on his otherwise smooth, tanned face. "You don't have a sire to recommend you to the duke—"

"You don't have a sire. Who recommended you?" I folded my arms and leaned my back against the front door, projecting far more casual calm than I felt. I was hungry again, and that hunger was laced with anxiety. It was a weakness I was determined to keep hidden, especially around Roman. I didn't need another lecture on the importance of setting up a blood harem or drinking directly from the source.

"I'm not a vampire," he answered, earning a sarcastic eye roll from me. "But I am half-sired, so my potential sire vouched for me."

"Who *is* your potential sire?"

Roman's frosty eyes dilated, and his breath hitched. It didn't seem like it should have been such a touchy subject, but it clearly was for him. He licked his lips as if working his way up to the answer. Then Collins arrived, just in time to offer up a distraction.

Collins parked his cruiser in the street. Roman's SUV lined the curb on the opposite side of the road, and my cruiser filled the driveway. It almost looked as if my house were about to be raided.

I pushed away from the front door, but Roman held his hand up to stop me.

"It would be best if you let me handle this alone." His

shoulders squared when he realized that I was trying to decide whether or not I would listen to him. "You won't like what I have to say, and your reaction will blow the cover story I've spent the last month building for you."

*Month?* My mouth dropped open, and I gaped at him.

"Just like that." Roman snorted. "See, you have no poker face."

He turned and stepped down off the porch to go greet Collins, leaving me behind, stunned and still reeling from his confession. Had he really known it would come to this for a full month? And I'd thought my self-esteem was sinking before.

Roman met Collins at the curb before he reached my front lawn. They stood just inside the beam of the cruiser's headlights, their shadows stretching down the asphalt road. Collins left the vehicle running. It hummed over their low voices, making it difficult for me to pick out their words.

I quieted my breath and strained to listen. Remembering Roman's jab about my poker face—or lack thereof—I turned my back to them and looked at the front door so Collins wouldn't see how I reacted to whatever I managed to overhear. My brain was too panicked to fathom what terrible thing Roman planned to tell him to get me off the hook.

"The captain will want to see some sort of documentation on that," I heard Collins say.

"And he'll have a copy of it by the end of the week, once I finish tying up this investigation."

*Shit.* I'd missed the meat of their exchange, and now it was practically over. That was fast. I glanced over my shoulder to get a better look at Collins' expression to see just how convincing Roman's story had been.

His gaze met mine, and he froze, revealing the storm of emotions swirling in his eyes. A dimple appeared on one side of his mouth like it always did when I knew he wanted to say more but was afraid to. It was the same look he'd had on his face when we were teens, and he'd asked me to go to prom with him when what he'd really wanted to tell me was that he was gay. I'd been so bummed about Vin not asking me to go, and true to form, Collins had come to my rescue. Or he'd tried to, anyway. I'd turned down his offer and skipped prom altogether, choosing to sulk over Vin instead—while Vin had been busy losing his virginity to Laura, thinking she was me.

So, my sister wasn't perfect. So, our relationship had a few near-fatal crashes. Laura and I weren't just twins. We were the only family either of us had left. It felt good to have her in my life again, sketchy past and all. Especially now that my weird new reality hindered my already dismal social skills.

I'd never tell Collins, but he could probably guess that I didn't have many other friends. Besides occasionally having dinner with him and his husband Lazlo, the only people I'd socialized with outside of work had been Will and his family. I'd spent my holidays with them after Mom died, during the years that Laura and I weren't speaking. That was another wound that had never really healed.

With the holiday season growing closer, and Laura returning to California, I wondered if we'd actually stay in touch like we kept promising. Would we make plans to see each other? Or would we settle back into old habits and burn the rickety bridge we'd only just begun to reconstruct?

Like I didn't have enough reasons to sweat the holidays as it was. How would Thanksgiving dinner go over when I couldn't actually eat anything in front of Alicia and Serena? Alicia's pecan pie was award-winning. She would be shattered if I turned down a slice.

I'd already stepped on Collins' toes by declining his dinner invitations for the past few months. Our friendship was on the rocks, and it made me wonder if the look he gave me now wasn't him deciding to wash his hands of me altogether. It hurt my heart to think that's what things had come to, and it hurt even more trying to accept that it was probably for the best.

Collins finally broke our gaze. He gave Roman a curt nod, then headed around the front of his cruiser. As I watched him climb inside and drive off, Roman made his way back to the porch. The chirping of crickets grew louder as if they had been eavesdropping, too, and now they were as curious as I was, wondering out loud all the possibilities.

"Well?" I said before Roman had finished climbing the front steps.

He gave me a pitying look, his blue eyes sincere. "He was a personal friend?"

I swallowed and nodded. "What did you tell him? Is he going to get in trouble for not bringing me in?"

Roman sighed and took the last step up onto the porch. "I told him that you were placed on the K9 unit by the FBI as an internal informant to investigate the claim that a white supremacist hate group had infiltrated the police force—"

"As a mole?" I covered my face with my hands. "You can't be serious."

"So the FBI—or Blood Vice, rather—will be paying all of the department's expenses for the extra training *Star* received, since she's one of *our* agents and was placed along with you for the investigation's credibility."

"And you've been building this cover story for a month?" My face was on fire. "You've known all along that I wouldn't be able to pull this off."

"It would be a challenge for any new vampire," he said, making a pained face as he watched mine twist up with humiliated rage. "If it makes you feel any better, I'm impressed that you made it work for as long as you did."

"Right. And if I hadn't made it work?" I snapped. "Were you waiting to spring into action, to *put me down,* as you called it? If I wasn't useful to your current case, is that what you'd be here to do right now? Damage control?"

Roman's sigh bordered on a growl. He closed his eyes and ran a hand down his face. "I'd forgotten what a pain in the ass you can be. Thanks for the reminder."

"That's not an answer—"

"No, I would not be here to put you down," he hissed. Then he leaned in and lowered his voice. "I didn't even report your involvement with the Scarlett Inn case."

"Why?" I had to crane my neck back to maintain eye contact with him. This close, I caught the scent of his skin— wet grass and cocoa butter. It was one part sedative and two parts aphrodisiac. I was pretty sure he knew it, too.

Roman watched me, waiting until the tension eased out of my face before he spoke next. "Everything I've done since we met has been an effort to keep you out of trouble, to shield you from the fate you'd undoubtedly face otherwise."

"Why?" I asked again. My voice was barely a whisper this time, rasping laboriously as I breathed in his intoxicating aroma. I was growing more docile by the second. "Why are you protecting me?"

Roman sighed and broke eye contact, twisting his head to one side to pop his neck. "It's my job to keep peace within the supernatural community, and this is the only way I can do that without having to…put you down. I don't particularly enjoy doing that. So this is me, being a nice guy. Try not to make it such a difficult task."

I swallowed and struggled to recall what I'd wanted to ask him before I'd gotten so offended. "How do I apply for Blood Vice?"

"You don't," Roman said. The trace of softness in his expression vanished. "I told you, you need a sire for that."

"But you don't—"

He held a finger up in front of my face. "If we're really going to have this conversation *again*, can we at least take it inside so we're out of your neighbors' earshot?"

I huffed and pushed the front door open. "After you."

Laura had left the light above the kitchen sink on. The soft glow spilled into the dining room and lit a narrow path across the hardwood floor, leading us beyond the dark hallways that cut through the center of the house and converged in the living room. I stepped lightly, hoping not to rouse Laura or Mandy.

Once in the kitchen, I fetched a bag of blood out of the refrigerator. I couldn't take it anymore. Surely Roman didn't expect me to have a harem put together so soon after his last lecture.

"Would you like something to drink?" I asked, attempting

to be a proper hostess before slurping down some cold B-positive.

Roman put a hand on the back of a barstool and gave me a hesitant look. "A glass of water would be nice."

"Sure."

I opened a cabinet and pulled down one of the new water goblets Laura had insisted we get for our upcoming dinner with the Bankses. I'd grumbled my way through the shopping excursion, but in retrospect, it was long overdue. And I was really glad to be offering the broody agent a drink in something other than one of the scuffed up, cartoon-inspired glasses that my mother had collected from half a dozen fast food joints for Laura and me as kids.

I filled the goblet with ice and water at the fancy new refrigerator and handed it to Roman. Then I took a step back and bit down on the bag of blood. Mandy, Laura, and Vin were used to watching me eat, and they'd stopped gawking so much. Under Roman's scrutiny, my awkward discomfort made a comeback.

"None of the vampires I work with consume pre-drawn blood. Is that…any good?" Roman frowned at me and took a careful drink of his water.

I snorted and pulled my teeth out of the plastic long enough to offer it to him. "Do you want a sip?"

He shook his head. "Human blood doesn't do anything

for half-sireds. Only vampire blood works for us."

I finished off the blood in record time and turned to deposit the spent plastic in the trash can under the sink. "You never did tell me who your sire is."

"*Potential* sire," he corrected me. "They're not a true sire until I rise as one of the undead."

"So, how's that work?" I asked, circling the counter and him to take the far barstool. His hand still rested on the back of the other stool as if he couldn't decide if sitting down would be a good idea or not.

"I've been assigned to three different vampires over the past fifty years." Roman cleared his throat and tugged at the collar of his turtleneck. "When I'm turned, my sire will be the most recent vampire who anointed me."

"Anointed?"

"Whoever's blood is freshest in my system," he added, seeing my confusion. "Right now, that vampire is my partner, Vanessa."

"But it wasn't always her?"

Roman pressed his lips together, and his frown deepened. "No. Just for the past twenty years."

"And before that?"

"The vampire who pulled me into the fold died a long time ago," he said softly.

"So what do I have to do to get on Blood Vice?" I asked,

steering the conversation back on course and away from the sensitive subject of his sire track record.

Roman sat up taller and heaved a sigh. "You don't have a living sire, nor a dead one you can safely claim, and if that weren't enough, you are an unregistered vampling."

"You keep saying these things as if you think I know what they mean." I held up my hands. "I'm not stupid, but I spent my human life learning a different set of rules for a different playing field."

Roman ground his teeth. "Sorry. I'm not used to introducing others to this world. Let me try again. If House Lilith were aware of you, they would have taken pity and put you out of your misery. Vamplings rarely survive their first year without the guidance of a sire. They consider it cruel and inhumane to let them blunder their way through the world alone until they self-destruct. It's also a waste of resources, sending Blood Vice to babysit when they should be heading off more sinister threats."

I twisted in my seat and raised an eyebrow at him. "Babysitting? Is that what you're doing here?" I waved a hand between us.

His mouth quirked up in a lopsided grin. "You've required significantly less babysitting, which is possibly another reason why I've gone soft and decided to spare you."

"Gee, thanks."

"Don't mention it." He gave me a pointed look. "I mean that. I could lose my job."

"So how do I get around the sire problem?" I asked. When his expression went stony again, I added, "Come on! There *has* to be a way, a loophole of some kind. I have a law enforcement background. Doesn't that count for something?"

"Your background is with a different set of rules. You said so yourself."

"Don't tell me there's no crossover usefulness here." I narrowed my eyes at him. "Who's wasting resources now?"

Roman shook his head. "I knew I would live to regret this. I just didn't think it would happen so soon." He shot me a resentful glare, but it lacked fire, so I took the opportunity to pout my bottom lip at him. "There *might* be a chance I could find a final death record for a nearby vampire you could claim as your sire."

"Really?" I perked instantly.

"Don't get your hopes up. It's a long shot," Roman said. "And if I do find a good candidate, you're not to ever mention I know anything about them. This lie will be yours alone to bear."

"Deal," I answered too eagerly, earning a frown from Roman.

"I don't think you understand how badly this could go—

for both of us—if you screw this up."

I folded my hands over my heart and tried to rein in the smile threatening to break my face. "I need this. I won't screw it up. Whatever it takes, I'll do it."

Roman didn't look entirely convinced. He sighed and took another drink from his glass before pushing it across the countertop. "I'll be back here tonight with my partner so we can go over the operation details beforehand."

"Tonight?" The Bankses were coming over for dinner, and I really wanted to see them, even if for only a short spell afterward.

"Is that a problem?" Roman asked, his shoulders pulling back as he stood up taller. "I thought you just said whatever it takes."

"Tonight is perfect. What time?"

"Ten."

That was more than enough time to visit with the Bankses. I practiced that poker face Roman didn't think I had and refrained from sighing my relief. Instead, I stood and walked him to the front door.

"I'll be ready with bells on," I said.

Roman gave me a dry smile. "Don't fuss over the bells too much. Vanessa will be dressing you for the assignment."

*Assignment.*

This was really happening. I was going to do a job with

people who knew what I was, and I didn't have to hide it or hold back. Adrenaline tinged my blood, and I had to bite down on my bottom lip to keep from cracking another dopey smile as Roman left.

It wasn't my mom's department, but maybe that made it even better. I was still trying to do good in the world. I liked to think that she would have approved of my effort. And I could have guessed what Dr. Townsend would have to say about the switch.

It was time to make my own mark, and I had sharp new fangs just for the occasion.

# Chapter Eight

It wasn't until Roman left that I remembered he hadn't told me about the pay for this single assignment. With the lingering possibility of a full-time position, I'd completely forgotten to ask again. I had enough set aside in savings to hold me over for a while, but it wouldn't last forever. I'd be sure to ask again tonight.

"That went better than I expected," Mandy said. She stood in the mouth of the hallway leading to her and Laura's shared room. Her messy, ash brown hair was knotted in a bun on top of her head. She still wore the wrinkled shorts, but she'd pulled on a cropped hoodie. Laura liked to keep the AC at a nippy sixty-five degrees. Duncan poked his head out of the pouch of the hoodie. Mandy blushed and shrugged at my surprised confusion.

"Laura's taking him with her in two weeks," she said as if that explained her sudden need to befriend the pooch. The drastic changes underway were getting to her, too, I realized. Why else would she be coddling a Chihuahua she'd threatened to eat at least twice a day for the past few months?

"Roman's going to find a way for me to join Blood Vice," I said, barely containing a squee of joy.

"Yeah, maybe." Mandy tilted her head to one side and gave me a hopeful smile.

"As soon as I'm in, I'll pave the way for you, too. If that's still what you want."

Mandy shrugged. "I don't know. They probably run background checks, and I am just eighteen. It would probably be best if I headed to Spero Heights. I've been mooching off you long enough."

"What?" I balked. "Mooching? That's not what you're doing. Who said that?"

"Me. I said that." She snorted and headed around the corner into the kitchen. I followed her, waving my hands in protest.

"You're not a mooch. A mooch is someone who doesn't do anything to contribute. You come to work with me every day," I said.

"And it's been great—mostly—but what am I going to do if you can't get me on Blood Vice?" Mandy opened the refrigerator and dug out a plastic punch bowl of pasta salad. She set it on the counter before turning around and using the heels of her hands to pull herself up on the ledge, too.

Duncan squirmed inside the pouch of her hoodie, twisting around until he was on his back, looking up at Mandy as she peeled back the plastic wrap over the pasta. He whimpered until she dropped a saucy noodle into his mouth.

I slumped on a barstool and chewed at my nails. "I was serious about mowing the lawn," I said. "There are plenty of things you could do around here, around the neighborhood, to earn some extra cash."

Mandy shrugged one shoulder. "Yeah, I guess. I'm just going to miss feeling like I'm doing something important, you know?" She reached over the edge of the counter to dig around in the silverware drawer, coming away with a fork. Duncan yipped again, and she fed him another noodle before stuffing her own face with pasta.

"I don't want you to go," I confessed. "I know I'm not your mother, and you can do whatever you want, but I like having you around. I like working with you."

"I know. I am pretty fantastic, aren't I?" Mandy gave me an ornery grin. "I like working with you, too."

The alarm on my watch buzzed. Sunrise was fast approaching, and I wasn't ready for it at all. I was still wearing my uniform—which would have to be returned with everything else the police department owned.

"Go turn into a pumpkin," Mandy said, shooting a knowing glance at my watch.

I grimaced. "Would you mind helping Laura load up all of the equipment and return it at some point today?" She rolled her eyes but nodded, her mouth too full of pasta to summon a reply. "Thanks."

I slipped out of the kitchen and down the hall to my room, unbuttoning my shirt along the way. After I gathered the rest of my uniforms and looped their hangers over my closet door, I had just enough time to pull on some PJs, brush my teeth, and tuck myself into bed.

My cell phone rang a few minutes shy of sunrise. I could feel the coming day like a weight on my eyelids, but when I saw Vin's number, I had to answer.

"I am so sorry," I blurted before he could say a word. "Ricker called in sick, and I had to cover his shift."

"Oh, of course," Vin said. There was a note of hurt in his voice, even under the relief. "I just wanted to check in before you crashed for the day. Were you able to help Agent Knight with his case?"

"Yeah. Well, I think so. I hope so." I wasn't sure how much I should be sharing about the investigation, and I didn't really have enough time to get into it right now. "Are you excited for dinner with the Bankses tonight?"

"I can't wait," he said flatly as if suppressing a groan.

I knew he was eager to be involved in the intimate dinner with people I considered family. The Bankses had nothing to do with Vin's discomfort. It was the idea of playing pretend with Laura that made him cringe. She wasn't thrilled about it either, so that made three of us. But it was necessary to pull off the event, since asking the Bankses to come over after eight, and then not actually eating dinner with them, would just be too rude.

The sun grazed the horizon, and I felt myself slipping.

"Jenna?" Vin whispered through the phone. "Are you still there?"

"Hmmm?"

"It's almost time. We should hang up."

"Okay." I couldn't hold my eyes open anymore.

"Jenna?"

My mouth wouldn't cooperate. There was so much more I wanted to tell him, but I could barely hum a reply. A gentle whisper of a laugh trickled through the line.

"Sweet dreams, Jenna," Vin said. Then he ended the call, and I died with the dawn.

# Chapter Nine

I woke Monday night with all the panic of a kid who had overslept on the first day of school. I'd expected this, though. Laura and I had planned and prepared for it. For weeks now.

I threw on a pair of jean shorts and a light gray blouse just before Laura burst into my room. Red wine stained the front of the shirt and shorts we'd decided to sacrifice for the occasion. She pulled out the feather earrings she wore and handed them to me.

"You're up," she said. "Alicia was just talking about joining a gym and a church choir to help keep her busy while Serena's off at school. I haven't said anything about you quitting your job—or anything about your work in general. Oh! Agent Sexy Pants sent someone from the FBI to collect your work crap and squad car and return them to the department, so I didn't have to. Also," she added with a furrowed brow, "Mandy is acting squirrely tonight. Even worse than Vin."

"Huh. Anything else?" I hooked the earrings through my lobes and turned for the door.

"Yeah. I ate pie for you," she said, crinkling her nose. "It was amazing, and I think I'm going to die."

"Ugh." I dragged my hands down my face. "That's so unfair. I think I'm going to die, too."

Laura stripped off the wine-stained shirt and dropped it into the hamper by the bathroom door. She wore one of my old sports bras underneath, unwilling to ruin one of her designer brands with our little stunt.

"I'll just be in here, doing crunches until I pass out," she said.

"Have fun." I slipped out of the bedroom and hurried down the hall.

Through the sliding glass door in the dining room, I spotted Vin sitting at the table on the patio. Alicia sat across from him with her back to me. Her shoulders trembled with laughter at something Mandy said, and Serena's musical chuckle made my breath catch. It was so good to see them in higher spirits.

White string lights hung from the pergola overhead, spiraling down the posts. They reflected off Vin's glasses as his head turned and he spotted me waiting inside. His eyes lit, and he stood up from the table, grabbing a few empty plates.

"I'll be right back," he said, pulling open the glass door. He set the empty plates on the counter and joined me on the opposite side of the dark room. His hands reached for my arms, but then he hesitated. The feather earrings had caught his attention.

"Is it really you? Tell me something Laura wouldn't know," he said.

"Long division."

Vin blinked stiffly but then nodded. "True enough."

"Did everything go okay?" I whispered, glancing over his shoulder and through the sliding glass door again.

"Everything is going great." He rubbed his hands down the backs of my arms and leaned in for a chaste kiss. The smell of pecan pie was on his breath. I hummed against his lips and frowned as he pulled away.

"I'm going to have something to *drink*, and then I'll be right out," I said.

Vin nodded and headed back outside. I left the kitchen lights off as I snuck around the counter and cracked open the refrigerator door.

As per my and Laura's plan, she'd removed the bags of blood. If she'd stuck to that plan, they were in an iced down cooler in the garage—all except for two that she'd emptied into a pair of rinsed out tomato juice bottles.

I downed one, swallowing loudly in my haste. Then I reached for the second bottle. My hand froze on the cap. At this rate, I would be out of blood before the week was over. I'd been drinking more and more lately. It was getting harder to resist overindulging. Any little bit of exertion or irritation sent me running for the refrigerator.

Roman's remark about requiring half as much if I drank from the source came back to me, and I harrumphed. He'd also mentioned that none of the vampires he worked with drank bagged blood. Would they think less of me if they found out I did?

Even if I did work up the nerve to bite Vin, Roman made it sound like one source wouldn't be enough. If I tried to drink from Vin every night, he'd be anemic in no time. I would never ask Mandy—and she'd already made it perfectly clear that wasn't an option anyway. Who else was I supposed to ask to do something as significant as open a vein for me?

The question roused my anxiety, and before I knew it, I'd drained the second bottle of blood. My stomach grumbled as if requesting more. *Shit.* That would have to wait. I'd taken long enough. I threw the bottles away and sucked in a deep breath before joining everyone on the back patio.

The table was littered with the remains of dinner and dessert. Vin had cleared away a few of the plates. The ones left behind held a scrap of salad or a pile of chicken bones. A sweaty pitcher of tea sat in the middle of the table, next to an empty bottle of wine.

Alicia glanced up as I claimed the seat beside her. Gray ringlets framed her face, contrasting with her rich complexion. Her high cheekbones were sharper than I remembered. She'd lost weight since the funeral.

"There you are," she said with a warm smile. "I was about to finish off your wine."

"Go ahead. I clearly don't need any more." I smoothed a hand down the front of my shirt and forced a smile despite the awkward blush heating my cheeks.

It felt all wrong lying to her, even if it was the right thing to do. Alicia had lost her husband. Exposing the dark truth behind his death wouldn't bring him back. It would only put her and Serena in danger. Just being in my life probably put them in danger, but I didn't have the heart to turn away from them. My life had been lonely enough.

Mandy gave me a strange smile. Then her eyes darted back to Serena. "So you want to be an architect? Don't they build houses?" she asked, resuming the conversation I'd interrupted.

Serena fingered a braid lying over her shoulder and grinned. "Yeah, but they also build other things like the Gateway Arch and the Louvre. That's what I want to do."

Alicia squeezed my hand under the table. "Mandy is a doll. Your mom would be so proud of you," she whispered.

"Thanks," I whispered back. A lump worked its way up my throat.

"How cool would that be?" Mandy said to Serena. She propped an elbow on the table and cradled her chin in the palm of her hand as she listened to Serena talk about her favorite architects.

Laura had somehow convinced her to put on something

more respectable than a ratty garage sale tee shirt. Instead, she wore a green off-the-shoulder blouse and a pair of khaki capris. She'd even curled her hair. Her eyes sparkled as she listened to Serena, and I couldn't recall ever seeing her look so genuinely excited—even though I was pretty sure she didn't have a clue what the Louvre was.

Vin finished off his glass of sweet tea and chomped on a piece of ice. "You know, Washington University, right here in St. Louis, is one of the top-rated schools for architecture."

Alicia's eyebrows rose up her forehead. "And don't they know it. Their tuition is almost five times as high as Mizzou's. Even with Serena's scholarship, we can't afford what they charge."

"Oh." Vin blushed, realizing too late that he'd touched on a sour subject.

"Don't get me wrong," Alicia continued. "I'd love for Serena to go to a closer school. In fact…" She paused and licked her lips. "I might be putting the house on the market soon and looking for an apartment in Columbia. It's only an hour and a half away. This city has just gotten too violent for me."

I pressed my lips together and nodded, not trusting my voice. My circle was getting smaller and smaller. Vin's hand rested on top of mine, grounding me. I still had him. Before it was all said and done, he might be the only one I had left.

"I love road trips," Mandy said, still cupping her chin and ogling Serena. "An hour and a half is nothing, especially if there's more pie involved," she added.

Alicia laughed and squeezed her shoulder. "Child, you look like you could use a few more pies in your life. Is our Jenna not feeding you enough?" She gave me a playful smile. "Growing girls gotta eat."

"Oh, she eats just fine." I smirked at Mandy's flushed face. She wasn't used to being fussed over or talked about like an average teenager. She wasn't an average teenager at all, but Alicia couldn't know that. We were both playing that awkward game called *normal* tonight.

Serena gave Mandy a sly grin, almost as if she was glad someone else her age was present to share the burden of being a teenager suffering the company of adults. Usually, a look like that from me would have prompted Mandy to roll her eyes or stick out her tongue, but not with Serena. She returned the girl's smile with a toothy one of her own. I realized I'd never seen her interact with someone her own age and chalked her odd behavior up to that.

"I thought you were on the K9 unit," Serena said, casting a wide glance around the yard. "I haven't seen your dog all night."

Mandy blanched at the comment and straightened in her chair.

"She's at the doggie spa," I said, giving Mandy another teasing grin. "I'll pick her up tomorrow after they buff her toenails and brush her teeth."

Laura had actually taken Duncan to some fancy doggie spa for the night. We were worried he wouldn't keep quiet through dinner, and if the Bankses spotted him, it wouldn't be hard to figure out that Laura was visiting, and then the ruse would be compromised. So, doggie spa it was.

I refrained from saying much more about work. I knew I probably should have shared that I was no longer with the department, and it was only a matter of time before word would get back to Alicia. Still, I didn't want to spoil the night by bringing it up. I hadn't even told Vin yet. I already knew what he'd have to say, and I didn't want to argue with him tonight.

Serena picked up her fork and pushed around the sliver of pie crust on her plate. "Did you graduate from around here?" she asked Mandy.

"Uh…no." Mandy's wide eyes turned to me. It was such a normal question, but she was panicking. She wanted to impress Serena. That was obvious enough.

"School records got mixed up with all the moving around she's done," I said, coming to her rescue. "We're still researching GED options."

Mandy sighed, but I could tell she wasn't thrilled with the

idea. It was one I'd pitched to her a few times before. If she wanted a better occupation than odd neighborhood jobs, she would have to give getting a GED some serious thought.

I had no doubt she could pull it off. She'd done just fine going through the K9 manual. If it were a matter of motivation, the embarrassed glance she gave Serena seemed like a spark I could throw some kindling on.

"Do you know what you want to do after you get your GED?" Serena asked.

Mandy shrugged. "I don't know. Maybe I'll go into law enforcement like Jenna. I like helping people."

Alicia cleared her throat, and her eyes glassed over. "There are lots of ways to help people. Lots of safer ways, too."

"I know," Mandy said with a nod. "But the safe ways don't protect kids like me from predators on the streets."

"You'll need more than a GED to go into law enforcement," Vin said. "And you have to be at least twenty-one to graduate from the police academy."

"One thing at a time." I squeezed his hand. "GED first. We'll worry about the rest when the time comes."

Mandy gave me an appreciative smile and turned back to Serena. "I already know a lot about the K9 unit. I helped train Star," she boasted. I didn't correct her. It was truer than either of us could actually admit.

"It's getting late." Alicia held up her hand to look at the watch on her wrist. The crystal cuff had been a birthday gift from Will. I'd had dinner at their house the night he gave it to her. I'd helped Serena make two dozen cupcakes—far more than the four of us had any business eating—all topped with an obnoxious amount of rainbow sprinkles.

Alicia eased her chair back and stood. "Thank you for the lovely meal. We should do it again soon. Maybe over Labor Day weekend. Serena will be home for a few days."

I stood, too, and hugged her. "That sounds nice." I couldn't tell her that would never happen, but I didn't know what else to say. So I postponed the disappointment.

Mandy, Vin, and I walked Alicia and Serena through the house and out the front door. I was about to call the evening a win and pat myself on the back, but then I spotted Collins' cruiser parked between Vin's green Beetle and Alicia's blue Honda. He was in uniform, likely on break.

"Max." Alicia beamed and offered him a hug as he met her in the driveway. "Always good to see your handsome face." She patted him on the arm and then turned to wave goodbye again.

Serena was already at the car, waiting eagerly at the driver's door. Alicia shook her head, but she climbed in on the passenger's side, relenting and turning over the keys to her daughter. I imagined she wanted to get in as much driving time as possible before taking off for Columbia, if she were still planning to take the Honda with her.

Collins at least waited for them to pull away from the curb before he turned his attention back to me. He nodded to Vin and blinked at Mandy. I'd never properly introduced them—not while Mandy was in human form anyway.

"Don't tell me you're being called into work again," Vin said, his voice thick with disappointment.

Collins overheard him. He paused in front of the porch steps and scoffed. "Not by me," he said. "Not by the county PD ever again either."

I winced at Vin's shocked face. "I didn't want to say anything while the Bankses were here, but I turned in my resignation last night."

"That's not all you did," Collins injected. "How long have you been a snitch for the FBI? Was it just since you've been in the K9 unit, or longer?"

Vin snorted as if Collins accusation were a joke.

"Just since the K9 unit," I said under my breath.

Vin's mouth dropped open. I grabbed his shoulder and steered him back toward the front door before he could say anything too damning. This wasn't a conversation I wanted to have out in the open, and I would have really preferred to go over the details with Vin before having to lie my ass off to Collins.

"You owe me an explanation," Collins shouted as we retreated back into the house. "We've been friends since the sixth grade. You don't get to shut me out of your life for no good reason."

"You want an explanation?" I hissed. "Then you're going to have to come inside for it."

"Fine." He stomped up the stairs and into the living room behind Vin and Mandy. I followed and closed the front door behind me.

# Chapter Ten

I'd never considered my mother's house tiny before, but with the four of us crowding the stretch of space just inside the front door and behind the sofa, I was suddenly claustrophobic.

"You don't need me for this. I think I'll head to my room," Mandy said, dismissing herself.

"Room?" Collins gave me a strange look. "Since when do you have a kid living with you?"

"Foster kid, and a few months now," I answered. Vin knew this shtick. He nodded his head in confirmation when Collins frowned at him, though he still looked bothered by the most recent reveal.

"Why wouldn't you tell me something like that?" Collins gave me a crushed frown.

What could I say to him? My solution to the discomfort I felt at having to lie was to avoid sharing those lies as much as possible. Which wasn't a great solution, but it was the best I could do.

"I've had a lot going on, Collins." I ran a hand through my hair and tried to use the small truth to soothe my shame. "Obviously, I couldn't share with you or anyone else that I was working for the FBI."

"But a kid?" He pointed his hand toward the hallway

Mandy had disappeared down.

Laura suddenly appeared in the mouth of the opposite hallway, the laundry basket tucked under one arm.

"Shit," she said through clenched teeth as she forced a smile at Collins. "Max! How are you?"

"Laura?" He blinked at her and then turned his incredulous eyes back to me. "And you definitely didn't tell me that your sister was visiting—or that she's a blonde again." He gasped, and I thought he might keel over. "You!" He pointed at her. "You've been running with Laz and me. I knew something was off! Jenna would never eyeball my husband's ass as brazenly as you do."

"Hey!" Laura and I said at the same time—her at him, and me at her.

"Some actress you are," I snapped.

She dropped the laundry basket and folded her arms. "I thought it would be ruder to *not* acknowledge his effort. And you never said I couldn't look."

"Wait, wait, wait." Collins shook his head. "*Why* is your sister running with us and not you? You're an FBI snitch. You've got a kid. Your sister has taken over your workout routine. What the *hell* is going on around here?"

The doorbell rang, and my anxiety went into overdrive, washing my vision with red.

"They're early. Fuuuck," I groaned and clenched my fists

in frustration.

"Who's early?" Vin asked, peeking through the front blinds.

"The FBI." I swatted his hand away from the window. "I *do* actually have to work tonight. I just haven't had a chance to tell you."

Collins scratched his head and huffed. "I'm here as a personal friend, not to hinder an FBI investigation. Unless, of course, you've been undercover since the sixth grade."

"I told you it was just the K9 unit," I said, clasping my hands together to draw everyone's attention. "I have top secret work to do with the FBI tonight, so all of this"—I circled a finger in the air—"is going to have to wait."

The doorbell rang a second time, and I answered it before anyone could say another word.

Roman and Vanessa stood side by side under the yellow glow of the porch light. Even in plain clothes, they gave off an ominous vibe.

Vanessa's hair hung in a slick ponytail high on the crown of her head. Her black blouse was sleeveless, showing off taut arms. Charcoal slacks hugged her athletic legs. She was a few inches taller than I recalled, but she wore heels tonight—open-toed, black stilettos that I would have no doubt broken my neck in.

Roman was the matching Ken to her gothic Barbie guise.

He wore black slacks and a gray, satin dress shirt. A giant duffle bag was slung over his shoulder that I guessed contained whatever Vanessa required to prepare me for the assignment.

"Are we interrupting?" Vanessa asked, her brows drawing together as she shot a quick glance around the room. Vin, Collins, and Laura gaped back at her.

"This is official FBI business, Jenna," Roman said, sounding none too pleased.

"You said ten." I looked across the room at the clock on the living room wall. "You're half an hour early."

"This was a mistake, Roman," Vanessa said, taking a step back from the door.

"No! It's fine," I insisted. "Please, come in. I was just seeing everyone else out." I waved my hand at Collins and Vin while Laura scooped up the abandoned hamper and headed off for the laundry room. She gave Vanessa an appreciative once-over as she went. I guessed she didn't see many women like that outside of Hollywood.

I ushered Vin and Collins out onto the porch and down the front steps. Collins stalked off toward his cruiser, not waiting to hear anything else I had to say. Vin was less pissy, but not by much.

"We *really* need to talk," he whispered, eyeballing Roman and Vanessa over my shoulder. "Soon."

I nodded and kissed his cheek. "Soon, but not right now," I said. "I'll call you in the morning."

Vin blinked a few times before wandering off to his car. As he opened the driver's door, he paused and gave me a tight, humorless smile. I had a feeling our pending phone conversation wasn't going to be a fun one.

I felt bad about not being able to properly break all the news to him, but there were only so many hours in the night. I was hoping that would improve as the days grew shorter. Maybe we could have something that more closely resembled a real relationship.

I returned Vin's smile, hoping he could see how sincerely sorry I was. He loaded into his car and headed off, leaving behind only Roman's SUV parked in the driveway. It looked less menacing there, almost as if it could belong in my quiet little neighborhood. The tinted windows hid the elaborate police package that spanned the entire dash within, and the four puck antennas spaced across the top of the vehicle were hardly noticeable against the solid black paint job. I wondered if I'd get a similar ride upon joining Blood Vice.

"She's too young, Roman. I don't know about this," Vanessa said under her breath as I turned around. Roman's lips pressed together in a tense frown as if he might agree with her.

"Vanessa, wasn't it?" I said, forcing a smile as I climbed

the porch steps to join them. "You were at the barn raid. And the scene last night, of course. We haven't been formally introduced. I'm Jenna." I held my hand out to her.

"I know who you are," she said.

For a second, I thought she might not take my hand. But then her cool fingers clamped around mine, and she gave a textbook shake. A tremor rocked my shoulders, and I blew out the breath I'd been holding as she pulled away. This was my first encounter with another vampire that didn't end with them biting me. The look on her face told me we were far from friends, but I still considered it a vast improvement.

Roman's expression relaxed after the exchange. I wondered if he, too, thought the greeting might end in bloodshed. I also wondered just how much he'd told Vanessa about me. There were too many secrets and lies going around to keep track of.

"Let's take this inside," Roman said, stepping through the front door I'd left open.

I waited for Vanessa, attempting to be polite, but when her green eyes widened, and she cocked her head toward Roman, I went ahead of her without hesitation.

*Don't mess this up,* I silently begged myself. I was sure it would be my mantra for the night. Vanessa had the sort of dry, abrasive personality that didn't take long to rub me raw. Kinda like Roman.

Potential sire, indeed.

# Chapter Eleven

Roman had made it perfectly clear that I would be playing bait. What he'd conveniently forgotten to tell me up front was that I'd be playing bait in a vampire nightclub. *Bleeders*. I don't know what I'd been expecting, but it hadn't been this.

Strobe lights and disco balls spun over the dance floor, casting a blanket of starlight over the mass of bodies gyrating to some funky beat that I didn't actually mind. I bobbed my head in time with the song as I wandered through the crowd, making my way toward the bar area in back.

Mirrors stretched over every wall, making the warehouse room appear far larger than it actually was and scattering the dizzying light show. It also made my gawking less obvious as I gathered my bearings and took in the show.

There was a general techno-goth look to most of the patrons, but every now and then I spotted a little something else. A Cleopatra in a toga dress. A manic pixie dream girl in bubblegum pink rubber boots and glittery hair extensions. A lumberjack with a gnarly beard and an unbuttoned shirt, showing off a ripped chest. The vampires were less obvious and flashy, and I found myself seeking them out more than anything. Were they all as intense as the few I'd encountered? Was there anyone here as lost and confused about this whole undead business as I was?

There were far more humans than vampires in the club. I could tell from the different colored admission bracelets. In the lobby, next to a poster displaying the dress code and rules, another poster outlined what the colors meant. The vampires in the club were given black bracelets, but the humans were divided into three categories.

Red was for professional donors open to solicitation. White marked those who were part of a blood harem and not to be approached. And yellow meant they were amateur donors and only available to experienced vampires who were less likely to overindulge and cause a problem.

As I made my way through the club, I noticed that many of the patrons dressed to match the color standards. Vanessa had made sure I matched, too. I fingered the black bracelet on my own wrist and squinted in the flashing lights to read the club motto printed on the paper. *Succumb to your dark desires and bleed the night away.* It seemed hokey, but apparently not cheesy enough to scare away too many humans, as evidenced by the hundreds of living bodies pressed in around me.

A few hungry eyes glanced at my wrist as I struggled through the crowd. I felt the urge to cover the bracelet, but Roman had said I was welcome to eat while I was here—as long as I stuck to someone with a red bracelet. It would help solidify my cover. He avoided talking about my bagged blood habit in front of Vanessa, for which I was grateful.

"Try one of the older women near the bar." Roman's voice buzzed through the tiny earpiece tucked down in my left ear. "Offer to buy her a juice first, and don't forget to ask if she has a preference for where you bite." I couldn't picture him frequenting this place on his days off, but I refrained from asking how he knew all of this.

Sweat coated my palms, and my stomach rolled. My fangs felt heavy in my gums, swelling with anticipation. What if I started drinking from someone and couldn't stop? Maybe this was a bad idea, but I didn't want to give Vanessa any more reason to question my competence, and I wasn't supposed to talk back to Roman's instructions for fear it would blow my cover.

The earpiece was already crammed deeper into my ear canal than I was comfortable with, but Vanessa had said it was necessary to prevent anyone with extra acute senses from overhearing. Apparently, that was a thing with certain vampires, especially the older, more experienced ones.

The crowd thinned as I reached the bar, and I was able to see myself in the mirrored display stretching behind the counter. Despite my worried expression, I fit right in.

Vanessa had teased and pinned my blond hair up into a fauxhawk fit for a runway, and she'd powdered my skin until it was even whiter than the perpetual night had rendered me. Dark coal outlined my eyes, and two stripes of shiny bronzer cut across one cheek bone. Pale lip gloss reflected the busy lights. I looked nothing like myself. Not even Laura wore this much makeup.

The black top I wore was snug, with one intricate lace sleeve that stretched down my right arm. My left arm and shoulder were bare, exposing a sharp collarbone that highlighted my reedy frame. I'd lost weight since becoming a vampire, but that wasn't so surprising. I was hungry all the time.

A few commercial juicers rested on a wide counter behind the bar, in between baskets of fresh fruits and vegetables. Two coolers stocked with sports drinks and mineral water were sandwiched in the far corners. Muscled bartenders in sleeveless dress shirts with bowties raced back and forth, filling tall hurricane glasses with custom juice concoctions. A waitress dropped off a tray of empty glasses at one end of the bar and gathered up another round before disappearing into the crowd again.

At the opposite end of the bar, a curvy woman in a red flapper dress and a feathered headband lounged on a barstool. Her graying finger curls were smooth, ending near her jawline. She was somewhere between forty and fifty. The throwback style and flashing lights made it hard to pinpoint a more precise age. A red bracelet slipped down her arm as she reached up to touch a delicate finger to the side of her mouth, smoothing the edge of her bright lipstick. She caught me staring and grinned.

"I haven't seen you in here before," she said, rolling the straw in her glass between her lips.

"Can I buy you a drink?" I asked, jumping right into the dialog I'd rehearsed.

"Definitely." She sucked down the rest of her beverage and waved a hand to flag down a bartender. I tried not to fidget as I waited, but the situation seemed about as classy as soliciting a prostitute.

The woman ordered a pineapple, orange, and carrot juice. I paid the steep twelve dollars without complaining and then followed her into one of the partitioned booths that lined either side of the club. The ceiling of the booth was open, letting in the sparkling lights and giving the bouncers outside a reflective view of our activity in the mirrored wall stretching above us. Black velvet curtains enclosed the booth, fading into the leather bench that ran seamlessly around the three interior walls.

"I'm Lydia," the woman said. Her soft voice was clearer behind the dark curtains that muffled the dance music. She set her glass of juice on a small table in the center of the booth before perching herself in a corner. Then she crossed her legs and stretched her arms across the top of the leather bench on either side of her. "You can bite wherever you'd like."

"I'm Jenna," I rasped, struggling to get the words out around my elongating fangs. "I enjoy drinking from the wrist."

I thought I heard Roman suck in a sharp breath through the earpiece as I inched my way closer to Lydia. I sat on the bench beside her and swallowed hard, trying to slow my panicked breath.

"Oh, honey," she cooed. "You're shaking. Is this your first time?"

Roman's voice lit up my eardrum again. "No, you do this all the time."

"No," I parroted him. "I do this all the time."

"Good," Roman said. "Tell her it's just been a while."

"It *has* been a while," I whispered, thinking more of Roman than Lydia now, but she seemed convinced enough. "And you smell so good."

She did smell nice. Her perfume was some mixture of jasmine and honeydew melon. It wasn't the tang of summer that rolled off Roman's skin like steam and made me want to melt into a puddle in his lap like I had the night he saved my life. But that was probably a good thing. I didn't want to mutilate her.

"Just go slow," Lydia said, sidling in closer to me. She wrapped an arm around my shoulders and lifted her opposite wrist to my mouth, stopping an inch shy of my lips.

She'd done this before. It showed in her calm confidence, even as she bubbled with excitement. I could see it in the way her pulse throbbed in the vein just beneath the swell of her palm. She wanted this as much as I did, and I couldn't understand why. I'd been bitten twice now, and neither time had been especially pleasant.

Maybe a gentle touch made all the difference. But the longer I hesitated, the less gentle I thought I could be. I was ravenous—damn near foaming at the mouth. My breath rushed out in a feverish pant, causing Lydia to pull away.

"I don't mind opening flesh if that would be easier for you, doll." She reached down the front of her dress and withdrew a small switchblade. She popped it open and lightly dragged it across her wrist. Blood welled up from the shallow wound.

I cupped the back of her hand as she returned it to me and kept my eyes lowered, too embarrassed to look up at her. The line of blood thickened, turning purple before it began to run around the curve of her arm. A drop splashed onto the knee of my black leggings. Still, I hesitated.

This was pathetic, and I was wasting time that I should have been using to find a serial killer.

"Nice and slow," Lydia whispered, snuggling in against me.

I took a deep breath and stuck my tongue out, lapping it

along the trail of blood and across the break in her flesh. It was liquid fire in my mouth compared to the cold bilge I sucked through torn plastic every night. The texture was silky, and the flavor rich. It sent goosebumps over my skin, and an involuntary purr escaped me as my lips suctioned onto her wrist, drawing more blood up through the cut.

Lydia's breath grew heavy as she squirmed beside me. I felt her breast press up against my arm, her hardened nipple pushing through the thin fabric of her dress and grazing my skin as my tongue prodded her wound. Her blood trickled down my throat, and my body warmed instantly.

The boiling sensation in my gut was not unlike the aftermath of a stiff drink. And just like an alcoholic, I wanted *more*. I sucked harder at her wrist, my fangs teasing the surface of her skin. Lydia hissed a sound that straddled pleasure and pain.

An alarm sounded in the back of my mind, growing louder the longer I drank. I ignored it, even after Lydia's arm went limp over my shoulders, and she stopped squirming beside me, having reached some climax I was nowhere near. Her fingers trailed up the side of my neck, a gentle encouragement to slow down. Or, more likely, to stop. I knew I should. Part of me even wanted to. I just…couldn't.

The way fresh blood affected me was beyond concerning. I was sure that was part of the reason I resisted it so adamantly. The fear of killing someone was always there, of course. But beyond that, there was an addictive quality that filled me with shame. And the lack of control terrified me.

Lydia's blood made me feel like a grape being rehydrated, injecting me with life and energy. I was under the spell of it, lost in a trance I couldn't break. If Roman hadn't intervened, I might have very well killed her.

"Jenna," he snapped in my ear. The tone of his voice told me it wasn't the first time he'd called my name. "The suspect is heading for the back with a female vampire. Are you listening to me?"

My fangs retracted. "Suspect?" I said out loud, forgetting what the hell I was doing there in the first place.

"Jenna—" Roman began, but Vanessa's voice cut him off.

"We don't have cameras in the back lobby, and we can't raid the place without a warrant. Snack time is over. Get your ass out there, now."

"Got it." I stood so abruptly that Lydia flopped onto her side behind me. I tossed a fifty dollar bill onto the table next to her drink. "Is that enough? This is my first time here…"

"What?" She blinked slowly at me, still fuzzy from the blood loss. I tossed another fifty beside the first one. "Sorry to suck and run, but I have to go. You were great," I added before bolting from the booth.

Everything was different—was more than I remembered—beyond the curtains. My senses were alive, my body humming with magic and unrestrained power as I cut through the crowd, moving as smoothly as a shark through water. And to think, some vampires did this every night. I felt like I could tackle an entire football team.

Whoever this suspect was had better look out.

# Chapter Twelve

There were a lot of things that Roman and Vanessa hadn't shared with me about the serial killer investigation. I mean, I get that I was the new kid on the block. I was also really desperate to make a good impression, even if it meant doing something as stupid as going undercover without all the facts.

I tried to recall the few things I did actually know as I came down from my blood buzz. Fact number one: eight of the missing vampires still unaccounted for had last been seen alive—well, however alive a vampire could be—at Bleeders, though it wasn't enough for a warrant, even by House Lilith standards. Fact number two: the club owner was not fond of Blood Vice, and he'd refused to give them access to the club's security footage. So they'd hacked his system the night before. Fact number three: the doorman was a former Blood Vice agent, so he knew exactly whom to turn away at the door. That's why I'd gone in.

I wanted to know more, but there wasn't enough time. Roman had calmed the worst of my nerves with the earpiece. I'd abandoned the rest of my doubts after Vanessa handed me a .380 loaded with the same pretty brand of ammo Roman had used at the barn raid. Silver Wolfsbane.

The brand was exclusive to Blood Vice, or so Roman had explained earlier in the evening while Vanessa gussied me up.

The bullets were made with wolfsbane extract and silver. The former was toxic to werewolves, and the latter was toxic to werewolves *and* vampires. The specialty ammunition would do more lasting damage against supernatural suspects than the kind of ammo I was used to working with.

Vanessa's outfit selection for me came with a strapless bra equipped with a front-access holster. I slipped my hand up the front of my shirt and wrapped my fingers around the stock of the .380 as I neared the back lobby of the club, leaving the light show behind.

The wall behind the bar reached all the way up to the ceiling, unlike the feeding booths, extinguishing the music and lights. The walls, floor, and ceiling were black, creating a foreboding darkness. My eyes slowly adjusted, and I picked out a few doors labeled as restrooms or storage. I worked my way from one end of the hallway to the other, only bumping into a herd of Elvira lookalikes exiting the ladies' room.

"The back lobby connects to the neighboring warehouses," Roman said in my ear. "The doors are usually locked, but a patron or two has picked their way into the furniture place on the south end for a bit more privacy. Try that side first."

I headed farther down the hall, my frustration building as the warm fuzzies from my encounter with Lydia slowly wore off. There was no southern door as far as I could tell.

"It's hidden behind the curtain," Roman prompted me.

The fabric hung in a smooth sheet against the wall, and I'd almost missed it in the darkness. I ran my free hand along the material, searching for an opening. My knuckles cracked against a bar of cold metal, and I gasped as it gave way, pushing into the room beyond.

"Hey!" someone shouted. I glanced over my shoulder and spotted one of the beefy bartenders. He stalked toward me. "That's a restricted area, ma'am."

I ignored his protests and ducked past the curtain.

The new room was dark, too, but an exit light in the distance outlined everything in red—rows of couches and armchairs covered in thick plastic, stacked headboards, and dining room chairs. For a moment, I wondered if my blood vision had kicked in. My pulse thrummed forcefully, but I suspected that had more to do with Lydia's blood than any fear of the bartender catching up with me.

A soft noise lured me deeper into the warehouse. I kept my hand on the stock of the firearm under my shirt, but I resisted the urge to draw it. If the suspect turned out to be some guy looking to neck on his girlfriend on the comfort of a plastic-wrapped mattress, there was a chance Roman and Vanessa would want me to come back another night— provided the bartender didn't have me thrown out. I'd snaked my way around a towering shelf of coffee tables by the time he entered the room. His fumbling arrival was noisy, and I was sure whoever I'd followed in here had heard him, too.

"This warehouse is not part of the club." His angry voice echoed through the room. "You're trespassing on private property, and if you don't cease immediately, I'll be forced to call the police."

He was lying. I knew from Roman that the hateful club owner didn't call the authorities in unless someone died—which was luckily a rarity, thanks to the professional muscle he hired to keep patrons in check.

A door creaked open on the opposite end of the warehouse. I wasn't sure what butted up against the other side of the furniture place, but that's where the suspect was making his departure. I gave up my stealthy prowling and hurried past a low row of dressers. The bartender caught sight of me from the next aisle over.

"Stop!" He jumped over a dresser and gave chase.

I could see the glowing exit sign now, and with my amped up senses, I could hear the buzzing hum of the bulb inside the fixture. I could even detect the sound of gushing water coming from somewhere beyond the door. I reached for the knob, but a strong hand closed around my arm.

"Busted," the bartender said. A menacing grin carved up his face. It didn't last long.

"Am I?" I pressed the muzzle of the .380 into his

stomach.

His eyes swelled, and his hand dropped away from my arm. He took a step back. "The police are on the way," he said, bluffing again. He was human, which surprised me. I don't know why, but I'd expected the club staff to be vampires.

"I am the police," I said. "And I wasn't the first one to come through here." I kept the gun pointed in his general direction and pushed the door open.

A half-full moon, hanging low in the sky, lit the alley squeezed between the furniture warehouse and the next building. It was hardly wide enough for a trash truck to access the dumpster next to the door—the open receptacle that assaulted my heightened sense of smell. I recoiled, but not before I caught the metallic scent of blood mixed with rotten produce.

"Oh, hell." The bartender paused in the doorway and gagged.

"How did the club's juicer scraps end up all the way over here?" I raised an accusing eyebrow at him.

"Our dumpster is full," he confessed. "I have permission."

"And a key?"

He slapped a hand to his forehead and groaned. "I must have forgotten to lock the door again. It's a pretty busy night, if you haven't noticed."

I held my breath and inched closer to the dumpster, peering over the edge. "So busy that you overlooked a dead body?" The gushing sound I'd heard before suddenly made sense.

The bartender rose up on his toes and peeked inside the dumpster. He jerked away so suddenly that he tripped over his own feet and had to catch his balance on the doorframe. "That wasn't there earlier. I swear!" He made another gagging noise.

"Jenna?" Roman's voice crackled through my earpiece, breaking up with static. He said my name again, and this time, it echoed farther down the alley. Then he appeared in the opening that fed into the front lot. An assault rifle was tucked in close to his chest, and when the bartender saw it, he darted inside the open door to take cover.

Roman's blue eyes landed on me, and his shoulders sagged with relief. "Down here. She's alive!" he shouted over his shoulder.

It was more than I could say for his suspect's latest victim.

The body in the dumpster was missing his head, same as the last body I'd found. And like that last victim, it had been stripped down and left somewhere the sun was more likely to reach first before humans.

The faded scars on my arm were all the reminder I needed of what the sun did to my kind. Whoever was killing these vampires wasn't looking for recognition. In fact, they were trying to hide their dirty work. This one marked the seventh victim that Blood Vice had found. How many more vampires had been reduced to nothing more than a scorched pile of ash after being beheaded and stripped over the past six weeks?

"So, are we thinking it was the woman you saw him with?" I asked, interrupting Vanessa as she ordered several agents to do a sweep of the back lot. She held a finger up in my face and turned to Roman instead.

"Get her out of my sight. Now."

"Excuse me?" My automatic response was half confusion and half outrage. Maybe it was the fresh blood still working its way through my veins that made me think I could square off with a stronger, more skillful vampire. Or maybe it was just stupidity. Vanessa clearly seemed to think so.

"You blew this one, vampling," she said, finally acknowledging me. "Not only were you no help at all, but you divided our resources, since Roman here decided we should confirm your safety before securing the perimeter." She shot him another lethal look before storming off.

"Hey, I did everything I was told to!" I shouted after her.

Roman grabbed my arm and tugged me down the alley toward the front lot. "You don't want to start a feud with that one. Not tonight. Trust me."

"That is such bullshit." I jerked my arm out of his grasp but kept moving in the direction he was steering me. "What the hell did she expect me to do differently? See through walls?"

Roman shot a careful glance over his shoulder. "I was under the impression that you could," he said in a hushed voice.

I was thankful for the copious makeup now. It hid the blush I felt working its way up my neck and into my cheeks. "That only happens when I'm overwhelmed, usually with anger or fear."

"And you weren't tonight?" Roman sounded surprised. He pulled off his stocking cap and opened the passenger door of his SUV. Surely, he didn't suspect I would retrace my steps down the alley to give Vanessa a piece of my mind.

I frowned at him and climbed inside the vehicle. "I felt too good after drinking that woman's blood to let the nastier emotions take over." It was the truth. I still felt good, like I could run a marathon around the city and not even break a sweat.

Roman closed my door and circled the SUV, stopping to deposit his rifle in back. Then he stripped out of his tactical vest before climbing into the driver's seat. Several agents were scattered down the street at various alley openings. Their black ops uniforms blended into the shadows, and I was sure they could make themselves near invisible if Vanessa ordered them to.

"I don't understand why she thinks *I* blew this," I said, folding my arms as I slumped in my seat.

Roman sighed. "Don't take it personally. She's more disappointed with me than you. I recommended you for the job, after all."

"Oh, that makes me feel so much better." I snorted and glanced out my window, trying to see down the alley we'd just exited.

"I called your name four times while you were in that booth," he said, a sliver of annoyance entering his voice. "The radio interference didn't become a problem until you went into the furniture warehouse."

"I heard you," I insisted. Heat filled my face again.

"Really?" Roman turned in his seat and gave me a dry smile. "Then you should remember the description of the suspect I gave you while you were in there." When I didn't respond, he started the engine and pulled out of the lot.

The angst and anxiety bubbling in my chest only grew worse as I stewed in a toxic blend of emotions. Shame and hopelessness pushed to the forefront as the spell of Lydia's blood tapered off. I bit my tongue, desperate to fix this mess I'd landed myself in, but not quite able to summon a solution in the wake of my epic failure.

"I'm sorry," I said after we'd traveled a few miles in silence.

Roman gripped the steering wheel and cleared his throat. "It's not your fault. It's mine. You're too fresh. I should have known better."

"I want another chance." I ignored the skeptical glance he shot at me.

"You're not ready," he said, following it up with a heavy sigh. "You can't even feed without losing your senses entirely. You should master that first."

The memory of the woman in the club made my heart burn like charcoal. "You told me to feed on the job. You said it would help with my cover."

"Yes, but you have to be able to do so while staying sharp and perceptive of your surroundings." When he noticed my dismay, he added, "Most vamplings struggle with that. It's the reason so few sires vouch for them until they've had at least half a century of practice. It doesn't help that you haven't been feeding properly to begin with." I flinched at the accusation before thinking better of it, and he gave me a humorless grin. "You won't stand a chance on Blood Vice if you continue to starve yourself. Not only will you be distracted and vulnerable, but you'll also be a liability to the core mission of the force."

"Which would be what, exactly?" I scoffed. "To make sure sleazy vampires get away with crimes for the sake of maintaining secrecy?"

Roman lifted an eyebrow and gave me a sideways glance. "If that's what you think we do, then why are you so desperate to be a part of it?"

I folded my arms and turned to look out the passenger window. He had me there. The truth was too embarrassing to give voice to. If I wanted any semblance of my human career—the career I'd strived to excel at and honor my mother with for the past decade—Blood Vice was my only option.

"Step away from your ego for a moment," Roman said as he turned the SUV down my street. "And really think about what would happen if humans were suddenly, as a whole, made aware of vampires and the like. Walk through that scenario, and tell me what the final outcome looks like to you."

I snorted and refused to look at him. I could do without his patronizing tone, but I had to admit, the hypothetical situation chilled my blood.

It would be mass hysteria. Widespread panic at best. There would be riots—probably on both sides of the fence. The human police and government would attempt to dismantle the vampire hierarchy, at least until they crossed the wrong vampire, and then it would be outright war. It wouldn't be over until the humans were reduced to nothing more than cattle. Or until every last vampire was set out to fry in the sun.

Roman caught my worried reflection in the windshield as we pulled into my driveway. "It will never happen," he said, sounding more reassuring than he probably intended to. "Blood Vice will make sure of it."

"Then that's a just enough cause for me to want in." I turned in my seat, giving him my full attention. "I want another chance. I'll do whatever it takes. I'll feed the right way, even if it means going back to that club every night."

Roman's shoulders tensed. "You won't be allowed back in that club. Your picture has likely been added to their black list already. Besides, do you really want to feed in a club where so many vamplings are going missing?"

"Then I'll find another club," I said, waving my hand. "This is St. Louis. You said there were thousands of vampires in this city. There have to be more clubs like that one."

"Don't you know any humans you can trust?" Roman asked. His crystal blue eyes turned up to me, filling with pity that grated on my shriveled pride. "That mutt would be ideal—"

"*Mandy*," I said through gritted teeth. "She's just a girl, and she's already made it perfectly clear that she's unwilling.

Also, I am not feeding on children."

Roman's jaw flexed. "And your morgue doctor? What about him?"

I sucked in a tight breath, and my eyes dropped down to the console between us. Any time I considered drinking from Vin, I thought back to the night Roman had dragged my broken body across the front seat of his SUV and cradled me in his arms before pressing his wrist to my mouth.

My heart hammered, and my cheeks filled with fire at the memory. I sensed Roman's sudden discomfort, too. When I glanced up, I could see the same memory playing out behind his eyes.

"I'm afraid of hurting him," I confessed.

"You'll have to get past that." Roman's voice had gone soft again. "You can't be afraid to live, Jenna."

"That's easier said than done, especially since I'm already dead." I smirked, trying to lighten the tense mood. Roman's serious eyes didn't stray from mine.

"Surviving as a vampire is quite an involved process, and joining Blood Vice entails a lot more than simple survival."

"Whatever it takes," I repeated, meaning it wholeheartedly.

Roman sighed and glanced out his window as one of my neighbor's cars grumbled to life. My wristwatch buzzed next, signaling the coming day. A purple haze lit the eastern horizon. It wouldn't be long now.

I waited, not wanting to give up for any reason, least of all for something as predictable and beyond my control as the sunrise. I felt like Roman was waiting for it, too. Waiting to let it dismiss me so he wouldn't have to.

"There's a house party," he said, squeezing the steering wheel with both hands. "Thursday night. It's being hosted by one of the duke's emissaries. Vanessa is a close, personal friend of his, so she and her harem—including me—have been invited. I don't normally attend these social functions, but Vanessa has asked that I go in her stead to offer an extra measure of security."

"You think Buffy will make a showing there?" I asked.

"Buffy?" Roman frowned at me. "We're not in the habit of giving serial killers pet names in Blood Vice."

I shrugged. "Sorry."

"But, yes, there is a slight possibility that the killer will target a party of this size." He inhaled a slow breath and pressed his lips together as he looked at me. "I'm allowed to bring a guest—"

"Yes," I answered before he could muster the nerve to ask. "I'll be your plus one. Pick me up at ten?" I asked as I opened my door. If I waited much longer, I wouldn't have the strength to make it inside the house.

"Jenna." Roman gaped after me. "This could be nothing.

I'm only offering so you have a chance to mingle with some of your own kind."

I nodded. "Sure, and I appreciate it."

"Good—"

"But if the killer happens to show, and I happen to help take her down, then that would earn me an interview for Blood Vice, don't you think?"

"Jenna." Roman sighed and ran a hand through his short hair.

"Is there a dress code?" I asked before he could launch into one of his broody lectures.

"Vanessa said cocktail casual, whatever that means." He grimaced. "And I'll pick you up at eleven."

"Eleven. Check." I gave him a small salute and closed the door, grateful that I still had the energy to manage the feat. My limbs felt like they were solidifying into blocks of ice, despite the muggy August air. I pressed a hand to the hood of the SUV as I walked around it and headed up the sidewalk toward the porch.

Roman rolled down his window. "Jenna?"

"Yeah?" I paused and glanced over my shoulder.

"Eat a proper dinner before the party."

The air rushed out of my lungs. I didn't know what to say, and even if I had, there was no time. I nodded and turned away from him, making my way to the porch as fast as my stiff legs would carry me.

Laura met me at the door. "Cutting it a little close, aren't we?" Her scowl disappeared when I fell into her arms.

"Help me to my room," I rasped. My eyelids were heavy, and I could barely keep them open. Laura grunted as I lost feeling in my legs, and she bore my full weight.

"Mandy!" she shouted.

If the girl were home, the two of them wouldn't have too much trouble wrestling me into bed. At least, that's what I was counting on. I wasn't going to be any help. The sun was up, and so was my time.

# Chapter Thirteen

I dreamed of the woman from the club. *Lydia.* It was the most vivid dream I'd experienced as a vampire, besides the ones that featured Roman.

Even though I knew right away that it was a dream—we were in the barn stall where I'd found Mandy after Scarlett's thugs had taken her—I felt enthralled by the call of Lydia's blood. She lay nude on the straw floor, beckoning me to join her with the crook of a finger.

I did, and I fed from her, but the taste of her blood was a shadow of what it had been in real life. Still, I drew from her as if she were a bottomless well, my hunger never quite dissipating. Desperation and panic filled me as much as her blood did. What if I couldn't stop? What if I was never truly sated again? What if I couldn't survive this horrifying new lifestyle without a sire?

I expected to wake covered in sweat and gasping for air, but as usual, my eyes simply blinked open, and I was some version of alive again, my senses and limbs slowly waking with the departure of the sun. Voices erupted in chaos around my bedroom, and I realized the lights were on.

Mandy's razor-sharp tongue was the first I recognized. "If you touch those fucking curtains, I will break your fingers. I'm not even playing. Try me."

"I have to call this in, Laura," Collins' strained voice was a surprise.

"Just five more minutes," Laura pleaded with him. "She'll be up any second now, I swear."

"This is lunacy." He sounded as if he'd been crying.

"You have no idea." I winced at his shriek and propped myself up on my elbows. Collins stumbled away from the bed.

"What the hell is wrong with you people?" He pointed a finger at me. "Do you think this is funny? Making me believe you were dead?"

"I am dead. Though I don't see how that's any business of yours."

Laura leaned against the doorframe, nervously stroking Duncan as he whimpered in her arms. "I tried to stop him, but he forced his way inside," she said. I was suddenly grateful that she'd never had to do any *real* work while filling in for me on the job.

"Trespassing, Collins?" I lifted an eyebrow. "What would the captain say?"

His finger stabbed the air again. "He wouldn't say jack shit because he fired me. Thanks to *you*."

From the brown pants, I'd assumed he had just gotten off work, though he'd already stripped down to the white tee shirt he wore under his uniform, and all the standard gear was missing from his belt, including his gun holster.

"I've been here, dead asleep, all day," I said. "How am I responsible for you getting fired?"

"I stuck up for you, like always, and I paid the piper for it today." Collins' face twisted with embarrassed outrage, his eyebrows lifting as they drew together. "I think I deserve better than a death prank."

My dry laughter only seemed to anger him further.

"I wish this were a prank," I said. "I really do."

"Jenna—" He clenched his teeth and closed his eyes before taking a shaky breath. "So help me, if you don't quit this nonsense, our friendship—whatever's left of it—is over. For good."

"You'd be safer that way." It pained me to say it, but it was the truth. If I really cared about Collins, I should've let him think I was a terrible person who pulled death pranks on the few friends gullible enough to stick their necks out for her.

Collins shook his head in disbelief. When he opened his eyes to look at me again, they were red-rimmed and glossy with unshed tears. "What have I ever done to you to deserve being treated this way?"

I sighed and glanced across the room at Mandy. She glowered at me.

"I am not a show dog you can command to perform tricks whenever it suits you." She folded her arms.

"I'm not commanding." I clasped my hands together.

"I'm asking. I'm *begging*," I added when her eyes narrowed.

Collins' eyes darted between us, confusion layering on top of the anger and sadness plaguing his expression. "Who is this kid? Child Services doesn't have a record of her placement with you. I checked."

"You checked?" I wanted to be offended at his snooping, but considering that his suspicions were well-founded, I didn't really have a leg to stand on.

Collins lifted an eyebrow at me as if to say *well?*

"You know her better as Star," I said, pushing the covers back and throwing my legs over the edge of the mattress. Lying down while everyone stood around looking somber and uneasy made me feel like I was on my deathbed. Which, technically, I was, but if I were going to take a chewing from Collins, I was at least going to do it at eye level.

He glared at me as I stood. "First, a death prank, and now you think you're going to convince me your illegitimate foster kid is a dog?"

"Wolf," Mandy corrected him. "Werewolf, if we're laying it all out now." She gave me another loathing glare.

Collins snorted. "And what about you, Laura? Are you secretly a unicorn?"

Laura's hand froze on Duncan's head, and she glanced at Mandy. "Do those exist?"

The girl shrugged one shoulder. "I've heard stories, but

I've never seen one myself."

"You people kill me." Collins shook his head and turned for the door. His lip curled up in a silent snarl when Laura didn't move out of his way.

"Glitter Sparkle Pants!" Mandy said suddenly, drawing a surprised breath from Collins.

"Excuse me?"

"That's what you called your husband on the phone," she said. "I overheard last week when you caught me peeing behind the station."

Collins' face flushed, and he swallowed as he shot me a hateful look. "Why would you share that?"

"Hey." I held my hands up. "I didn't share anything."

Mandy groaned at Collins' resistance and tried again. "You still chew nicotine gum, even though you hide it from everyone."

Collins teeth clenched, and his eyes bulged. He was becoming unnerved. I could see it in the square of his shoulders.

"You press the chewed globs to the underside of your desk. It's disgusting." Mandy stuck her tongue out. "I saw every time Jenna walked me through the station. It's a whole different, repulsive world when viewed from two feet off the ground."

"Are you part of the cleaning crew?" Collins squinted at

her. "Is that where I've seen you before?"

Mandy's shoulders sagged, and she growled softly. Then she stepped in closer to Collins and took a deep breath. "You ate fried chicken and had a cream soda for dinner, and—" a sharp grin sliced across her face "—and you had *relations* today."

Collins blanched. "Are you following me? What the hell is this?" He looked back to me for an answer. "Why do you have this girl tailing me?"

I sighed and crossed the room toward him, opening my mouth wide. As expected, he leaned away from me and made a face. Before he could ask what I was doing, I pointed both index fingers up at my exposed eye teeth. Then I forced them out of my gums the way I practiced when I brushed them.

"The fuck!" Collins stumbled backward and into Mandy.

"Watch it," she snapped. She gave him a shove and moved to stand in front of my open closet door.

Collins made to exit the bedroom again, and this time, Laura let him. I trailed behind as he fled down the hallway.

"Do you believe me now?" I called after him. "I didn't mean for any of this to happen, Collins. I swear!"

He didn't slow down as he rushed for the front door, tripping over the area rug behind the couch. He didn't reply either. It was as if a switch had flipped, triggering his fight or flight response. At least he wasn't trying to fight me. It was a small relief.

"You can't tell anyone," I said, reaching for his arm. He yipped and jerked away from me. His eyes were dilated, and he gasped each breath as if he thought it might be his last. "It could put you and Lazlo in danger. Please, don't tell anyone," I begged.

Collins turned to leave again, squealing when the doorbell rang. I put a finger over my mouth, trying to calm his panic, and peeked through the curtains.

"Shit," I hissed and jerked the door open. "I am so sorry I didn't call last night."

Vin stood under the glow of the porch light with his hands shoved down into the pockets of his khaki shorts. The pitiful look he gave me sent a stab of guilt through my chest.

"It's okay. Laura said you barely made it in before sunrise," he said with a half-hearted shrug that did little to disguise his disappointment. "I wanted to make sure you were okay and had plenty of blood."

"You know, too?" Collins had found his voice again. He stepped back to peer through the doorway at Vin. "Why am I the last to hear the news?"

"Probably because we all knew you'd freak out," Laura answered as she and Mandy joined us in the living room.

My sister was dolled up tonight. I had a sneaking suspicion that meant she was waiting on a call from

Hollywood. She caught my judging scowl and lifted her nose in the air. Now was not the time to bicker over her terrible taste in men, but we really needed to have that talk before she disappeared from my life a second time.

"I'm hungry," Mandy said, rubbing her stomach. Food was always her go-to when she wanted to excuse herself from an awkward situation. She took Duncan from Laura and headed for the kitchen. "Let's get us a snack."

"A *small* snack," Laura called after her. "He's gained a whole freaking pound this summer."

Collins made a strangled noise. "She's really a…werewolf?" he whispered, staring after Mandy.

Laura nodded. "But she sheds like a Sasquatch."

"I heard that," Mandy yelled from the kitchen.

Collins sputtered out a disgruntled sound. "This isn't normal. You can't make it all go away with some lame joke. This is *not* okay."

Vin stepped inside and closed the front door behind him. This wasn't a conversation for the neighbors to overhear, and I appreciated his attentiveness to my privacy. Collins had put the brakes on his hasty exit, but he lingered near the door as if he might change his mind at any moment and bolt.

"Aren't you supposed to be careful about sharing your secrets with too many of us mortals?" Vin asked. His smile was tighter than usual.

"Laura's a lousy bodyguard," I said, earning an eye roll from my sister. She threw her hands in the air and stalked off toward her and Mandy's shared room.

"Bodyguards actually get paid," she grumbled before disappearing around the corner.

"I guess that explains why she was running with Laz and me in your place." Collins' brow crinkled. "How did this happen? When did it happen?"

I thought of Will, and my heart dropped. It wasn't a story I wanted to tell again. Ever again. It hurt too much, like poking at a festering wound that refused to heal.

"A few months ago." I licked my lips and tried to summon a simple answer that would pacify him, but I just kept seeing Will's vacant eyes, and the blood pooling around his ashen face.

Vin touched my arm. "I think that's a tale for another time," he said to Collins. Then he nodded toward the kitchen and ushered me that direction. "You look pale. You haven't eaten yet, have you?"

"Oh, man." Collins waved his hands in front of his chest. "I don't think I'm ready for all that yet. This is gonna take some getting used to."

Vin shrugged. "It's just bagged blood."

Collins took several deep breaths and then reached for the door behind him. "I need some time to think this through."

"You can't tell anyone," I said, panic edging into my voice again. "It's too dangerous. There are…people who take care of humans who try to out my kind."

"Are you threatening me?" Collins lifted his chin. The fear bleeding through his eyes gave him away, no matter how hard he tried to hide it.

"It's not a threat." I shook my head. "At least, not from me. It's a warning. I don't want anything to happen to you."

Fear finally won out, and he dropped his courageous façade before rubbing the back of his hand under his eye to wipe away a runaway tear. "Who would believe me anyway?" He pressed his trembling lips together and gave me a short nod. Then he left without another word.

A sinking sensation gripped my insides as I wondered if I'd ever see him again. Is this how Alicia and Serena would react if they found out? Or would it be worse? Would someone like Roman be sent to take them out—before taking me out, too?

That was how it worked, to the best of my understanding. Vampires were regarded as ruthless because they had to maintain such tight control over their human harems, or else House Lilith would mark them as a threat to the community and have them put down. It was that simple and that complicated. I hated it, but what could I do? I was nobody. I didn't even have a living sire to explain all of this nonsense to me.

I stared at the closed front door, willing Collins to come back and forgive me for things I had no control over.

"Give him time." Vin rubbed my shoulders and steered me toward the kitchen again. "We're overdue for a long talk anyway."

Not exactly the comforting words I'd hoped to hear, but he was right. There was a lot we needed to discuss. None of which I was looking forward to.

# Chapter Fourteen

Vin was not tickled about me working with Roman. That much was obvious. There was a jealous streak there that I was afraid to touch. I could barely admit my attraction to Roman to myself. Admitting it to Vin was not happening. Not tonight, at least.

I sat at the breakfast bar beside my brooding doctor and sucked down a third bag of blood while he scrutinized me through his spectacles. He only wore his glasses when we were at odds. They were like his armor, a shiny token that made him feel more in charge. Kind of like my Glock.

"So you can feed off some trollop in a vampire bar, but not me?" Vin cleared his throat and folded his arms over the countertop. We were almost up to date. I hadn't mentioned the party Thursday night yet, but it could wait.

"She was a stranger." I licked the corner of the blood bag I'd just finished and hopped up to throw it away. "If I accidentally drained her, I wouldn't have felt half as bad as I'd feel if I did that to you."

Vin gave me a sheepish smile that conveyed his gratitude for my affection and his doubt all at the same time. "What about Roman? Were you not as afraid you'd drain him?"

I gave Vin my back as I turned toward the refrigerator again. Thinking about the incident with Roman did something to me I wasn't ready to share with Vin.

"Roman's experienced at giving blood," I said. "He does it all the time. Plus, I didn't have a choice. I was dying." I'd given Vin the same reasons every time he brought it up. I was beginning to feel like a suspect in interrogation, the detective just waiting for me to slip up and incriminate myself.

"You've had three already," Vin said softly as I fingered the waning supply in the door of the refrigerator. I hesitated and pulled my hand back.

"Roman says I have to put together a proper blood harem if I want to join Blood Vice." I blurted the sentence out in a single breath. It was the confession I was most dreading, but our whole conversation had been building up to it.

"Harem." Vin made a sour face and pushed his glasses up the bridge of his nose. "That's such an offensive word."

"Like trollop?" I lifted an eyebrow and leaned over the counter across from him, folding my arms to mirror his. "I can't just feed on you alone. That's not healthy or safe."

Vin grumbled, but he reached across the counter and took my hand, rubbing his thumb in nervous circles over my knuckles. "Who else did you have in mind?" he asked in a flat, guarded voice.

I blew out a heavy breath. "No one at the moment. I'll keep supplementing with the bagged blood until I figure that out. Baby steps."

"When do we start?" he asked in a very different voice, one that sent a nervous thrill through my midsection.

I sucked in my bottom lip and considered him a moment, searching his eager eyes for some sort of reassurance. If we did this, there was a pretty good chance we would end up naked, too. I was well aware of that. In fact, it seemed only fair.

Feeding on someone's blood was incredibly intimate, and I had a feeling Vin would want something other than the hundred bucks I'd thrown at Lydia. In retrospect, I had to wonder if I'd offended her. Roman hadn't given me enough to go on to know what proper etiquette was, and he'd probably been too afraid to offer more direction in front of Vanessa for fear she would discover just how new I really was.

The more I thought about it, the more sense "harem" made. I wondered if all vampires were sexually intimate with their blood donors. Then I wondered if Roman was intimate with Vanessa. The thought stirred up a nasty concoction of jealousy and embarrassment deep in my gut. I had no right to care about whom Roman gave his blood or body to—and certainly not when I had a warm, willing man right in front of me.

Vin squeezed my hands over the counter and tugged me in closer so he could reach my mouth with his. The swell of his bottom lip was still raw from where I'd accidentally bitten him. I ran my tongue across the healing cut, and he made a content noise in the back of his throat.

We were like nervous teenagers, kissing and groping and grinding, never quite taking that final plunge. I was no virgin, but I wasn't exactly experienced either. Just beneath the fear that I wouldn't be able to control my bloodlust was the more human fear that I wouldn't be any good in bed. I hadn't had sex since college. Since before my mother died.

Vin took his lips off mine long enough to tug me around to his side of the counter and pulled me between his parted legs. His erection was obvious through his khaki shorts. It pressed against my stomach as he wrapped an arm around me and kissed the side of my neck. His free hand slid up the front of my shirt and cupped my breast, my nipple resting in the dip between his thumb and forefinger. He squeezed, and the gentle pinching sensation drew a sudden gasp from me.

"Let's take this to the bedroom," I whispered.

Vin didn't have to be told twice. He stood, keeping his hands in place on my body, and walked backward out of the kitchen and down the hallway, kissing and touching and squeezing me the whole way. By the time we made it to our destination, I was ready to devour him.

We didn't take time to turn on a light, but my nerves triggered the blood vision, and the room faded into focus in shades of deep red. I watched the outline of Vin's body as he stripped out of his shorts and polo. He discarded them on the floor and felt his way through the dark and into my bed.

I followed slowly, stalking him like the predator I was. I left my tank top and shorts on. Vin had hung onto his boxer briefs. It was probably a good idea for now. If this went to hell in a hurry, we didn't need to be naked when Laura rushed in to help.

"Where are you?" Vin whispered, sliding his hand across the bedspread, seeking me out.

I'd circled around to the side he lay on and was staring down at him, trying to decide if I was really ready to go through with this or if I was rushing things because I was desperate to be on Blood Vice.

I decided I might be overthinking things as Vin's hand touched my leg. His fingers trailed up the inside of my thigh, and my mind was suddenly made up. I climbed onto the bed and straddled him, centering my hips on top of his. His breath hitched as I slowly leaned over, our bodies rubbing together as our lips met again.

My fangs were out, I noticed as Vin's tongue flicked against their tips. They swelled, elongating further and forcing my mouth open even more. Vin turned his head to the side, exposing his throat to me. His pulse throbbed just above his collarbone. A thin sheen of sweat rose up on his skin, and the scent of summer rose up with it, cocoa butter and cut grass.

It reminded me of Roman, and my gut tightened again.

"Jenna," Vin whispered. His chest rose and fell eagerly. "Do it, Jenna. Do it now."

The timing of the invitation tipped me over the edge. I closed the few inches between us and sank my teeth into the fleshy spot where Vin's shoulder met his neck. Blood filled my mouth in a hot rush.

I tried to compare it to my time with Lydia at Bleeders, tried to draw similarities between the way their bodies writhed with arousal—but the darkness and the scent of summer kept pulling my mind back to Roman and his shockingly blue eyes, his wrist pressed against my mouth.

Vin's body jerked beneath mine as his back bowed, thrusting me into the air, and he groaned blissfully. Dampness soaked through the front of my shorts. A pleasant warmth filled me—more from the blood than the friction between our bodies—but it was relief rather than disappointment that helped bring my feeding to a gentle close.

"Vin?" I said breathlessly. "Are you okay?"

"I'm in heaven." He whispered out a clipped laugh. "Maybe a little embarrassed. Was it—did you—"

"I'm good," I said quickly. "You were great."

"But you…didn't…" His voice trailed off, and I couldn't tell if it was more from exhaustion or humiliation.

"I got what I needed."

I rolled off of him and propped my head up on one hand, rubbing my other over his chest in lazy circles. With my fading blood vision, I inspected the marks I'd left on the side of his neck. They were small and neat, hardly seeping at all. I dabbed at them with my fingers, wondering if I should go find some antibiotic ointment.

A moment later, Vin's snores sawed through the darkness. I was wide awake. It wasn't even midnight yet. I had hours to kill, and nothing to do with the heady new blood coursing through my system. Or the guilt ruining my afterglow.

I'd bitten Vin, but Roman had been the one on my mind. I was pretty sure that made me a terrible person.

I didn't need anyone to spell it out for me. The half-sired agent belonged to someone else, and just because he was being nicer didn't mean he had feelings for me. He was being kind because he felt guilty.

Weren't we all?

# Chapter Fifteen

I changed my shorts before venturing into the kitchen to escape Vin's grizzly snoring. He'd never slept over before tonight. The idea of having someone in bed with me while I was dead to the world was just too awkward, and I didn't really feel like lying down during the few hours the sun allowed me to be up and about.

Out of habit, I opened the refrigerator, but as I stared at the row of blood bags in the door, I realized I wasn't hungry. The epiphany made my chest swell with gratitude and fresh guilt, and I was soon reduced to a sobbing mess.

I'd spent the majority of my short life as a vampire with an aching hunger that gnawed on me at all times. The absence of that suffering made me feel almost human again. And just like with Roman and Lydia, shame and insecurity quickly flooded in to fill the void.

"Oh, it's just you," Laura said as she came into the kitchen. She wore a silky, pink nightgown with overflowing cleavage. When she caught sight of my tear-streaked face, she froze. "What happened? Is everything okay?"

"I bit Vin," I said with a sniffle.

"Oh my God. Is he dead?"

"No," I sobbed.

"Are you upset that he's *not* dead?"

"No!"

"Did he leave you over it or something?" Laura cocked her head.

"He's still in my bedroom."

"And?"

"And I'm not hungry anymore."

"I've seen how you drink," Laura said. "Are you sure you didn't kill him?"

"Laura!"

"Then why the hell are you crying?"

I slammed the refrigerator door and threw my hands up in the air. "I'm not hungry anymore."

She blinked at me for a few seconds. "So…is this, like…a *good* cry we're having here?"

"Maybe. I don't know." I dragged my hands down my face. "He came when I bit him."

"Kinky."

I groaned. "Why is it so hard to have a serious conversation with you?"

"I am *seriously* confused. How's that?" Laura stepped around me to grab a diet soda out of the refrigerator.

I took a deep breath and tried to organize my thoughts before speaking again. "This just seems like a lot more commitment than I'm ready for. But I can't tell you how amazing it is not to feel like I'm starving to death right now."

Laura cracked open her soda and took a small sip. "Are you afraid of losing the blood delivery service? Can't tall, blond, and broody help you with that now that you're working together?" The mention of Roman summoned fresh tears. Laura sighed. "Did I miss something?"

"Roman has a sire—well, a *potential* sire. He only gives blood to her."

Laura's perfect eyebrows rose, and she gave me a sympathetic frown. "Oh, honey." She pulled out a barstool for me and took the one beside it. I plopped down with a dejected exhale and buried my face in my hands.

"What's wrong with me?"

"I get it." She rubbed a hand over my back. "I mean, it's obviously not the *exact* same thing, but I feel like I'm starving all the time, too. Comes with being a star in the biz." She sighed. "And I totally get wanting someone you can't have and settling for the next best thing."

I made a face and twisted on my barstool, pulling away from the comfort of her hand. "Vin is nothing like Hollywood. He would never cheat on me or set fire to my career. He's a freaking angel, and I think that makes it even worse."

Laura rolled her eyes. "David might not be a saint, but what he lacks in the angelic department, he more than makes up for with his bank account. When he screws the pooch, I get diamonds. When Vin's in the doghouse, what does he bring you? Flowers? *Blood?*"

"I don't want him to bring me anything. Well, okay, maybe the blood." I put my face in my hands again and shook my head. "He's the only one willing to open a vein for me, and I'm the shitty one who should be in the doghouse right now. I need him—and at least two more donors—if I want to make this work so I can get on with Blood Vice. I can't afford to be honest with him, no matter how much he deserves it."

"Good grief. You're just a glutton for punishment, aren't you?" Laura scoffed and took another drink of her soda. "And here I am, making an art out of using men to get what I want."

"Why?" I sniffled and wiped my face on the sleeve of my tee shirt. Laura tried and failed to hide her disgust, finally choosing to inspect her nails instead.

"It beats being a pitiful waif who's so blinded by nobility that she gets walked on all the time." She gave me a strained smile. "Not that that's what you are. It's just a lesson I had to learn early on to survive in my world."

"That's horrible, Laura."

She turned to look at me, sending her wave of blond hair over her shoulder. "I can see how it might seem that way from a distance, but David and I do love each other, in our own screwed up way." She smirked at my distasteful glare. "This isn't the first time we've taken a break, and it's not always him stepping out of line. The tabloids aren't as completely bogus as we all wish they were."

I'd never admit it to Laura, but I had a copy of every magazine she'd ever so much as been mentioned in. They were stashed in an old gift box under my bed. It was the only glimpse I'd had of her life for a lot of years. I was at least certain that half of the crap they said about her was not true, but the other half left me wanting to pick up the phone, though, in the end, I never did.

I shook my head, pitying my sister despite her efforts not to be pitiful. "I don't want a rollercoaster for a love life."

Laura shrugged. "Then learn to love the good doctor. He should keep things nice and stable and boring for you."

"Stable doesn't have to be boring." I refused to believe that. Maybe it was a rarity—in any world—but it didn't mean I was ready to give up on trying. Even as the newly dead, maybe *especially* as the newly dead, I needed hope in my life.

A long stretch of silence passed with Laura sipping her soda, and me sniffling and dabbing the snot and tears from my face with the hem of my tee shirt. Once my mild hysterics had dried up, Laura wrapped her arm around my shoulder and pulled me in for an awkward half-hug.

"I'm sorry life is sucking right now. I hope it gets better. For both of us."

"Me, too." I took a deep breath and returned the hug,

patting her on the back. Through the silky fabric of her nightgown, I felt a strip of metal clasps. "Are you seriously wearing a bra to bed?"

"No. I just finished a video chat with David," Laura said. "Had to make sure the girls looked their best."

"Gah." I crinkled my nose. "Can we change the subject to something other than our fucked up love lives?"

She snorted. "You asked."

"And I'm sorry I did."

"Fine." She slipped the straps of her bra down her shoulders and under the sleeves of her nightgown so she could pull her arms through before rotating the bra to unhook the clasps. "Tell me what happened last night that you almost got yourself fried like an egg on the front porch this morning."

Not exactly the lighter subject I was going for. I chewed my bottom lip, trying to decide how much I could and should tell her, and how to best condense it. "There's a vampire serial killer in St. Louis, and I screwed up and let her get away last night."

Laura's brow bunched. She extracted her bra from the top of her nightgown and dropped it on the counter before turning her full attention back to me. "That sounds like an awfully big job for a newbie. Did they really expect you to take her down singlehandedly?"

"Well, no," I stammered. "But I'm the reason she got away." I chewed my thumb nail. "I don't know if I'm going to get another chance to prove myself. If I don't, I'll be stuck with some shit job that will make me wish I was deader than I already am."

"But Agent Knight came to you," Laura said. "He asked for your help, didn't he?"

"Yeah…" I sniffed and reached up to tighten my ponytail. "I guess he wasn't offering a permanent position. Just a single assignment. That doesn't mean I'm going to stop pushing. There's still a chance I could help solve this case. I'm hoping that at least earns me an interview."

Laura frowned and tapped her fingernails on the side of her empty can. "You're not doing something that could get you in trouble with these big, scary vampires, are you?"

"No. Not yet, anyway." I gave her a tight smile. "But I am going to a party with Roman Thursday night. He thinks there's a possibility that this serial killer could show up there. If she does, I'll be ready."

The click of tiny toenails signaled Duncan's arrival in the kitchen. He paused at the counter and turned gloomy eyes up at us before letting out a low, mournful howl.

"I guess Mandy hasn't come home from her date yet," Laura said, giving the Chihuahua a pouty face. "No people food for you, Duncaroo."

"Date? What date?" How had I missed that? She must have slipped out of the house while Vin and I were having our long, uncomfortable talk in the kitchen earlier.

"She and Serena went to a late show at the movie theater," Laura said, glancing at the clock on the microwave. "Maybe they stopped to grab dinner afterward."

"Serena? Serena Banks?" I snapped.

Laura leaned back in her stool and blinked her wide, astonished eyes at me. "You couldn't tell what was going on between them at dinner?"

The idea of Mandy and Serena together was too much. I hadn't known either girl played for the home team, but that wasn't what bothered me. If Mandy and Serena became an item, it would only be a matter of time before Serena found out the truth. And then Alicia would find out. And then I'd die all over again.

"But they just met," I balked. "And Serena is going off to college. And she's my late partner's daughter. And Mandy is a werewolf!"

"What's that supposed to mean?" Laura slid off her barstool and circled the counter to throw away her empty can. Duncan followed, his tail wagging hopefully. "Is she only allowed to date other werewolves? *You're* dating a human."

"That's different," I said.

"How?"

"I require humans for sustenance."

"And Mandy doesn't." Laura gave me a berating glare. "Which, technically, means she's less likely to maul her dates than you are. So why shouldn't she be allowed to date humans?"

I ground my teeth together. "Let's try that subject change again."

"Fine." Laura snagged another diet soda from the fridge and cracked it open. "What do *you* want to talk about?"

"Thanksgiving."

Laura choked on her first drink from the fresh can. She coughed and hacked over the sink a minute before catching her breath. "Thanksgiving?" she rasped. "What about it?"

"We haven't had one together since Mom died."

"That's months away. Why is it even on your mind?"

I shook my head. "It just is. What do you and Hollywood do every year?"

Laura set her can down on the edge of the counter before wiping the corners of her eyes with her pinky fingers to clean up the mascara that had bled during her coughing fit. "Well, David doesn't have a lot of family that he's close with. His parents are dead, and he was an only child. So we usually take a mini-vacation to the Bahamas while the rest of the cast and crew are off with their families."

"Oh." Lots of sunshine, then. Great. Even giving up the

window seat on the plane wouldn't fix that one. "What about Christmas? What do you do for that?"

Laura cleared her throat. "It depends. Sometimes we do another vacation, and sometimes we stay at home and hit all the celebrity holiday parties." She pressed her lips together and fingered the lace collar of her nightgown. "The set goes dark for a couple of weeks around Christmas and New Year's. I could always fly back for a weekend to visit. We could do our own thing. It doesn't have to be on the holiday itself, right?"

"I guess not," I said.

Laura put a hand on her hip. "And it's not like you're going to care if there's a big, fancy meal prepared since you wouldn't be able to enjoy it anyway."

"That's not the point." My cheeks warmed, and my eyes burned, threatening to tear up again. "I've just missed you."

"I missed you, too." Laura gave me a lopsided smile. "We could always stuff an apple in Vin's mouth and make him curl up on a serving platter if that would make it more festive."

I snorted and grinned at that. Then I sobered as I thought of Alicia and Serena. "I'm going to have to come up with an excuse to bail on the Bankses. I hate to do it, but there's no other way."

"Tell them you're visiting me," Laura said. "When I come to town to visit you, I'll slap on a blond wig and have dinner with them one night if you want. Speaking of," she added. "I really need to dye my hair back, so the color has time to settle before shooting begins. Is that going to be a problem?"

I sucked in an anxious breath. This was it. No more daylight backup plan. I was on my own. The front door opened and closed before I worked up the nerve to answer Laura, and Mandy joined us in the kitchen, much to Duncan's delight. He yipped and danced happy circles around her feet.

"I'm starving," she announced on her way to the refrigerator, though a wide smile split her face nearly in two.

"Join the club," Laura said under her breath, earning another grin from me.

"Speak for yourself."

Mandy stuffed a plate of leftover chicken breast and mashed potatoes in the microwave before turning around to face us. "Is that lawn mowing gig still up for grabs?"

"As long as you don't plan on telling your new girlfriend any secrets you shouldn't." I narrowed my eyes at her.

"Right, because that would go over real well." Mandy snorted. "Sorry about the morning breath, babe. I was howling at the moon and licking my ass last night."

Laura made a horrified face. "You do that?"

"What? No." Mandy blushed, but I'd caught her a time or two. We all had our dirty secrets, I guess.

"Yes," I said to Laura. Mandy opened her mouth to

protest, until I added, "You can go ahead and dye your hair back for your soap opera."

Mandy's embarrassment faded, and her bottom lip slowly bloomed out. "You're really leaving? And taking Duncan Punkin away forever?" She bent over to scoop up the frantic Chihuahua and snuggled him in the crook of her arm like a baby.

Laura scowled at her. "I know you've just been fattening him up so you can eat him."

Mandy scratched Duncan's belly and wiggled one of his paws. "That's right," she baby-talked to him. "I'll eat you up, little toe beans and all." Then she looked up at Laura. "You better do that video chat thing with us like you do with that creepy old dude—with more clothes, of course, and puppy face." She held up Duncan for emphasis.

"That old dude is basically your uncle." Laura gave her a malicious smile that prompted the mother of all eye rolls.

"In what level of Hell?" Mandy asked, her tone lighter and more playful than I expected.

"You're in an oddly chipper mood," I noted, wondering just how well her date with Serena had gone.

"Is that a problem?" Mandy's cheeks flushed, and she shrugged one shoulder. Duncan licked her hand to encourage her to keep scratching his belly.

I shook my head. "I'm glad you're happy, and extra glad

that you're staying."

Mandy grinned. "Maybe change isn't all bad."

# Chapter Sixteen

After Laura and Mandy had turned in Tuesday night, I spent an hour doing pushups on the back patio. The exercise helped burn some of my pent-up energy, and, despite the fact that vampires were naturally stronger than humans, we apparently had to maintain our muscle mass the same, mundane way. So unfair.

An hour before sunrise, I crept back into my bedroom, careful not to wake Vin, and picked through my closet for something that said cocktail casual vampire party. Not surprisingly, I didn't have much to work with. My final choices came down to a blue pantsuit I'd worn to a department charity dinner a year ago, or a lavender summer dress Alicia had helped me pick out for Serena's high school graduation.

I thought of Vanessa and her classy, gothic style. Envy drip-brewed from my chest into my stomach again, and I fingered through my wardrobe once more in search of something black, tight, and sexy. Nothing.

It was too late to find something online since the party was only two days off, but maybe I could make it to the mall and find something that would work before they closed Wednesday night. I'd have to leave the house immediately after sunset. I set a reminder on my phone.

I woke Vin just before sunrise, officially ready to boot him out of my bed before I kicked off for the day. I didn't want to think about how traumatic it would be for him to roll over and spoon my cold body in the early hours of the morning. And I definitely didn't want to be the one to help him discover any deep-seated necro-fetishes he might have.

"What time is it?" Vin whispered, squinting in the light from the fire hydrant lamp on the night table.

"Almost six," I said, handing him his shirt and shorts. "Get dressed. I'll make you some coffee and OJ to…replenish your fluids."

Vin glanced down at his crusty briefs and winced. "Oh, wow. Last night was…"

"Intense?" I offered. He nodded sheepishly.

"I'm so sorry I crashed on you, especially after…"

"Don't sweat it." I headed for the door, hoping to hide my own awkward reaction. "I'm going to get on that coffee and OJ before the rigor mortis sets in." Oh, the things I'd never thought to hear coming out of my mouth.

"Thanks, babe," Vin called as I stepped into the hallway.

*Babe.* I cringed but didn't say anything. Either the high from his blood was wearing off, or I was just being moody and irritable because I couldn't have my cake and eat it, too. Not unless Vin changed his name to Cake.

I shoved my disdain and guilt to the back of my mind and

focused on setting up the coffee pot. I couldn't have a cup with Vin, but I still enjoyed the smell. It filled me with longing and nostalgia that stretched back as far as my childhood, when my mother had guzzled down a full pot every morning before taking off for her shift.

I could feel the sun creeping closer to the horizon, so I went ahead and set out a mug and the cream and sugar. Then I dropped a bagel on a plate and dug the tub of cream cheese out of the refrigerator before filling a glass of orange juice and adding it to the growing spread on the breakfast bar.

Vin joined me just as the coffee maker hissed its farewell note. He slid onto a barstool and gave me a shamefaced smile. His dark hair stuck out on one side, and his glasses looked slightly cockeyed on his nose.

"This looks great. Thanks." He peeled open the cream cheese, and I turned to grab a butter knife out of the drawer for him. "Thanks," he repeated.

"You should probably have some protein soon, too," I said, trying to recall what else we were told to eat after doing blood drives at work. "Maybe some steak and leafy greens."

Vin yawned and nodded. "Really, I don't feel half bad. How much do you suppose you drank?"

I shrugged. "Maybe a cup?"

Vin took a sip of his coffee and nodded. "So half of what I donate for one of your blood bags every week."

I frowned. "You've been drawing your own blood, too?"

"Of course." He blinked at me, confused. "Why wouldn't I?"

"I don't know. It's just…I didn't realize…" My voice trailed off.

It made sense, I guess. I wasn't sure why the thought of drinking his nameless, faceless students' blood didn't bother me as much. Ignorance is bliss? Now I felt like I should get to know them, maybe buy them dinner or something. Not that I could explain my mysterious gratitude without ruining everything.

Vin took a bite out of his bagel and watched me with calculating eyes. The scrutiny was less intimidating with his messy hair and cream cheese-laced mouth. My wristwatch buzzed.

"Time for bed." I circled the counter and gave him a chaste kiss on the cheek.

He swallowed hard and turned toward me for a real kiss that I managed without shying away from his morning breath. "I'll see you tonight?"

"I have some errands to run, so it might be late," I said, trying not to sound too relieved.

I liked Vin, despite my conflicted feelings for Roman, and I didn't want to hurt him. But I also needed some space to deal with all the noise in my head and to focus on figuring out how I was going to find the rest of this blood harem I needed to have in place like yesterday.

Vin nodded. "I have to be in early at work Thursday morning anyway. Maybe Thursday night?"

I pinched my lips together. "Maybe just for a bit. My next undercover assignment is later that night."

"You didn't say anything about that before." Vin's brow pinched.

"I just found out," I lied, not wanting to hash out the more honest reasons minutes before sunrise. My limbs were already growing stiff. I leaned over Vin and gave him another quick peck. "We'll still have a couple of hours Thursday night before I have to go."

He nodded slowly and gave me a pained smile. "Sure. That sounds great."

"Goodnight." I headed off for my bedroom before anything else could be said.

Vin was a good guy. I had to keep reminding myself of all the things he'd done for me. He was also attractive and intelligent and…stable.

Maybe Laura was right, and I was just craving what I couldn't have. I'd done a lot of that in my lifetime, and now I knew just how much I had taken for granted because of it. I didn't want to take Vin for granted, too. But that didn't stop my heart from wanting what it wanted, no matter how forbidden.

For now, that desire would have to wait. My first priority was getting a harem put together so I could convince Roman to somehow arrange an interview for me with this duke.

As I lay in bed, waiting for the sun, I thought long and hard about whom I could ask to do something so morbidly essential. Laura was moving back to Hollywood, Mandy was out of the question, Collins was freaked out, and the idea of the Bankses discovering what I was terrified me.

I wasn't sure what options that left me with. Maybe I could track down Lydia's number and see if she wanted to go steady. That wouldn't scream desperate at all. My only other choice was to ask Roman again about where to find a different vampire club, one that hadn't been frequented by Buffy these past few weeks.

As I ran out of ideas and was about to succumb to self-pity, the sun rose, saving me from myself.

The mall was quiet Wednesday night—except for Mandy's non-stop chattering. The girl was so bubbly, I began to wonder if I shouldn't search her room for a hidden stash of happy pills. I could use one about now.

I hadn't rested well. I'd gone to bed hoping to put some

distance between Vin and me, and instead, I dreamed of nothing but him. When the sun finally set, I'd woken feeling guiltier than a nun watching porn.

"Do you think Serena would like this?" Mandy asked, holding up a thick, glittery bracelet.

I grunted a sound that could be interpreted however she liked. "One date and you're already buying jewelry?"

"Yup," Mandy chirped. "Sometimes you just know, you know?"

I lifted an eyebrow and turned back to the rack of dresses I'd been scouring ever since we arrived. I wanted to look like I belonged at this party. More than that, I wanted to be the best-looking thing there. I wanted Roman not to be able to peel his eyes off me. Of course, that would probably make our job a little more difficult to manage. Decisions, decisions.

"Which one of these would stand out the most at a vamp party?" I held up a tight, strapless dress that looked more like an undergarment, and a lacy number with a thigh slit. Both were black.

Mandy's mouth tucked to one side. "You really want to stand out?"

When I nodded, she reached behind me and pulled a white cocktail dress off a rack. The cap sleeves and high collar were constructed of a loose-knit crochet, but the bottom was a silky material. It fanned out into a flirty skirt that fell mid-thigh. It looked like something an ex-girlfriend might wear to a wedding to piss off the bride.

"No way," I balked. Maybe taking fashion advice from a teen wearing cut-off shorts and a breakfast cereal tee shirt wasn't the best idea.

Mandy nodded firmly. "Everyone at that party is going to be wearing black. You know why? Because blood doesn't show as well on it. Wearing white is as racy as it gets for a bloodsucker. You would totally steal the show in this."

I considered her reasoning as a recorded voice announced over the speaker system that the mall would be closing in ten minutes. Mandy stole a glance at the bracelet display and shoved the white dress at me.

"I know bloodsuckers, but you know Serena," she said. "Which one?" She held up the chunky glitter bangle again and grabbed a leather cuff with braided detailing to model alongside it.

"The leather one." Mandy squinted at my hasty answer, so I added, "She's going to school to be an artsy fartsy architect. Total hipster."

Mandy tilted her head from side to side. "Fair enough." She put the other bracelet back and gave me an expectant look, waiting for me to make a decision on the dress.

"You'd better be right about this," I said, hanging up the two black gowns.

We checked out of the little boutique, and Mandy snagged a pretzel with cheese before we exited the mall.

My old Bronco sat by its lonesome in the middle of the parking lot under the glow of a security light. With the top off, it looked more like a truck or Jeep. As soon as we crawled inside, I opened the back window to let in some air. I really needed to get the air conditioner fixed, but I was putting it off, holding out hope for a fancy SUV like Roman's.

"I've been thinking," Mandy said as we buckled up and I started the engine. "Blood Vice might not hire me until I'm older, and mowing lawns is pretty seasonal work…" She paused to give me a serious look and tucked her mousy hair behind one ear. "How much would you pay me to be part of your harem?"

I took my hand off the shifter and left the Bronco in park so I could turn in my seat to face her. "Wow, that's… Wow." Knock me over with a feather. "I don't know about that, Mandy. You seemed so opposed to it before, and I'm still a total newb. Hell, I was worried about taking too much from Vin last night. It took two months to work up the nerve to bite him again after the first time."

Her cheeks flushed, and she looked down at her lap. "A different vampire drank from me every other day for nearly a year, and they weren't exactly gentle about it. If they'd killed me, Scarlett would have made them hunt down a replacement and called it a day."

I swallowed. "All the more reason why I would never expect you to bleed for me."

"I know you care about me, Jenna." Mandy looked up again and gave me a small smile. "You wouldn't have let me stay with you scot-free for the past few months if you didn't. You wouldn't have tracked me down in that barn—"

"That was my job." I shook my head. "And you're just a kid. You deserve to have someone looking out for you. You don't owe me anything."

Mandy's eyes unfocused, and she turned to gaze out the windshield. "I haven't been a kid for a long time."

"You know what I mean." I sighed and turned to look out into the darkness with her. "I'm not taking care of you because I want something in return."

"And I'm not offering because I feel obligated to."

We sat in silence for a few moments while I wrestled with the thought of feeding on Mandy. Roman had said werewolves were as good as two humans. But Mandy was my responsibility—maybe not exactly a daughter, but close enough that the idea of doing what I'd done with Roman and Vin with her seemed wrong on multiple levels.

The conversation wasn't over, but I had the feeling we both needed some time to absorb what had been said. I grabbed the gear shift and put the Bronco into drive, signaling a reprieve from the iffy subject, and pulled out of the mall's parking lot, heading for home.

# Chapter Seventeen

"You're sure about this?" I asked Collins.

We sat on the back patio under the lit-up pergola while Mandy, Serena, Vin, and Lazlo played cornhole in the dark, navigating by the light of the waning moon and a swarm of fireflies. Duncan ran back and forth, yipping his little head off in between snatching up unattended beanbags. It was such a normal scene, I could have almost forgotten that I was a creature of the night, if not for the subject matter of our hushed conversation.

Collins sipped on a bottle of beer and leaned back in his chair. I hadn't seen much of him outside of work lately, so the cargo shorts and plain tee shirt took some getting used to. He looked younger and less serious, especially with the light stubble sprouting up along his jawline.

"We've been friends since we were eleven," he said. "My feelings were really hurt at first—and I won't lie, it freaked me out. But…I get why you didn't tell me. I remember how long it took me to work up the nerve to tell you that I was gay."

"That was the week after graduation, if I remember right." I whispered out a nervous laugh even though there wasn't anything remotely funny about the heart-to-heart we'd had before college.

My mind was still doing laps around Collins' earlier offer,

one that echoed Mandy's from the night before. Mandy and I hadn't talked about it again yet. It seemed my desperate prayers had been answered, and I wasn't sure if I trusted the sudden good fortune. I'd been a skeptic for far too long. My heart wanted to swell three sizes like the Grinch's, but my brain kept screaming *Danger, Will Robinson!*

"The point is, I want to be supportive," Collins said. "I want to help, and maybe you could return the favor by setting me up with an interview for this…Blood Vice, was it?"

My eyeballs bulged so violently, I thought they might fall into my lap. "You want to work with a bunch of vampires?"

"You said some of them are human, right?" His forehead crinkled, and he gave me a questioning frown. "There's not another local police department that'll hire me after the bridge I just burned. I don't want to move, and I'd rather be working alongside you anyway."

"How does Laz feel about this?" I glanced across the yard to where his husband played beanbag tug-of-war with Duncan.

Lazlo Ramirez was the younger brother of Collins' former partner within the PD. And I thought *my* holidays were going to be rough. The very Catholic family had just accepted Collins as one of their own after six years, two of which he and Laz had been married. I imagined Laz's brother wasn't too happy with Collins right now either.

Laz was a pediatric nurse for a private family doctor. His income was nothing to sneeze at, but they liked to keep up with the Joneses. Their lifestyle couldn't be sustained on one income for very long.

Collins sucked down the rest of his beer before answering my question. "Laz is not thrilled that I went all flame-on and lost my job, but he's proud of me for sticking up for you. And no," he quickly added, "I haven't told him that you're a vampire. Though I did share that you're working with the FBI now, and that I hoped you could hook me up with a job there, too."

I winced. "I'm not actually working for the FBI. Not yet anyway. I was just an undercover civilian for a single assignment."

"So you weren't a mole looking to bust some hate group within the department?"

"Nope," I confessed.

"That's a shame. The place could have used a little house-cleaning."

"I had to quit because Laura is going back to Hollywood. But Langford thought he was going to keep Star—Mandy—and that wasn't happening. And I couldn't get arrested over it, for obvious reasons. So Roman helped me out with a cover story that fixed both problems."

Collins smirked and stood up from the table to grab

another beer out of the cooler he'd brought. "That Special Agent Roman Knight sure talks a good game, doesn't he?"

I kicked my feet up onto the table and folded my hands over my stomach. "He's got fifty years' experience with a department where he's required to lie his pants off to keep a lid on the most dangerous secret imaginable."

"And what nice pants they are." Collins sat down beside me and took a long pull from his new beer. "If I weren't a married man, I'm sure I could find a more enjoyable way to help him lose those."

I swallowed and kept my mouth shut, which was damning enough on its own. Collins gave me a knowing look, but to his credit, he didn't comment on my awkward silence.

"So blondie is a super old vamp?" he asked instead.

"He's actually human—well, sort of. He's half-sired, so that's why he looks so good for his age."

"Half-sired, huh?" Collins' brow creased. "How's that work?"

"He drinks vampire blood, so if he dies, he'll rise as one. Or after a hundred years on the force, he gets to…off himself and become one, I guess." There was probably a ridiculous ceremony or, hell, a marching band for all I knew.

"That would be weird," Collins said, running a hand over his jaw. "I wouldn't want to stay young forever. I like the idea of growing old with Laz too much, and if I turn into a vampire, I'm thinking his family will take it as their personal mission to hunt me down and stake me in the name of the Virgin."

I held my hands out. "No family is perfect."

He snorted. "I think I could learn to get along with vampires, though, and if I'm donating blood to you, the rest of them should leave me alone, don't you think?"

"I would kill them if they didn't," I said, surprising us both.

I'd meant the statement as a joke, but who knew for certain when dealing with vampires? If it came right down to it, I would kill another vampire before letting them harm any of my friends. No doubt. Dying hadn't robbed me of that principle. If Mandy hadn't already taken care of Raphael, I'd still be hunting his undead ass to exact justice for Will. Archaic vampire rules be damned.

"So, what do you say?" Collins asked. "Do you *vant* to suck my blood?"

I snorted out a quiet laugh and rolled my eyes. "How are you going to explain the bite marks to Laz? Won't that become an issue?"

He shrugged. "I'm sure we can get away with making a tiny cut that could be easily covered with a bandage. You don't actually have to sink your teeth into my flesh, do you?" He made a sour face.

"I don't think so, but I'm not an expert by any means," I said. "I've been drinking bagged blood mostly, but Roman says straight from the source is best. He didn't say anything about how it came out of that source." I felt the gums around my fangs throb at the prospect of a fresh meal, and my mouth watered.

It was almost ten, and I needed to be thinking about getting ready for the party. I had an uneasy feeling that Vin's backyard surprise party was meant to stall our feeding until the last moment. He was probably hoping to hang around and beat his chest like a territorial gorilla in front of Roman.

I'd stuck to bagged blood Wednesday night, and while I was feeling that nagging hunger in my gut once again, it wasn't to the point of full-on agony yet. Still, Roman had said to eat a proper meal before he picked me up. I had a feeling he would be able to tell if I didn't.

Collins stood and waved for me to follow him inside. The rest of the gang was too preoccupied with their game and Duncan's shenanigans to notice our departure. We slipped through the kitchen and down the hallway to my bedroom. Laura was tucked away in her room, video chatting with Hollywood, so the house was quiet.

"I should warn you," I whispered as Collins clicked on the light and closed my bedroom door. "The few people I've bitten and drank from have had pretty strong reactions."

Collins' eyes widened. "What? Did they scream? Piss themselves?"

"Vin jizzed in his shorts."

Collins made a strained face. "Well, that's better than pain, I guess. But maybe if you're not biting down, just drinking the blood as it drips out of my arm, it won't have that effect?"

I shrugged. "Your guess is as good as mine."

"What if I bled into a cup? It would still be fresh, yeah?" He made for my bathroom, and I followed, curious to see what this experiment would reveal.

My bathroom was a disaster. Mandy showered in the one she shared with Laura, but she still pilfered through my makeup drawer and borrowed my curling iron, especially after Laura'd had a meltdown the first time she touched her collection of designer hair gadgets and products.

Collins picked up a toothpaste-spotted cup off the counter and wiped it down with the hand towel hanging from the circular bar on the wall. I dug through the cabinet behind the mirror and found a pair of manicure scissors, some rubbing alcohol, cotton balls, and a bandage. I lined everything up on the counter.

The setup reminded me of the time we'd planned to pierce our own belly buttons when we were in the eighth grade, which really, probably should have been my first clue that Collins was gay. Looking at the similarities in our arsenals, I began to worry that the outcome of this might be just as horrifically unsuccessful. I wondered if we'd ever learn.

Collins chattered nervously as he cleaned the scissors and then his wrist with the alcohol. "You don't, like, freak out and go ravenous at the sight of blood or anything?"

"Not anymore," I answered truthfully. As long as I had my blood bags, I could muscle through any dark desires to maul and maim.

"Good," Collins said. "Not that I plan on making a big, bloody mess in your bathroom or anything. I just wanted to make sure."

My nerves were stoked by his excitement, and red pulsed at the edges of my vision. "I have bagged blood in the refrigerator if you change your mind," I said, taking a step back toward the door to give him some space.

"I think we can do this. It'll be fine." Collins took a deep breath, and then he opened the tiny pair of scissors and pressed the bladed edge down on the inside of his wrist.

I turned away as a slight queasiness pinched my insides. In the heat of passion, drawing blood didn't seem so…icky. But here, like this, was a little different. A second later, I heard a drip of liquid echo as it hit the bottom of the cup. Then several more followed. After what felt like forever, Collins finally nudged my shoulder.

"How's this?" he asked, handing me the cup. His dark blood filled it halfway. I swirled it around and gave it a sniff like I'd seen fancypants wine connoisseurs do on television. Then I downed it.

It wasn't as hot—temperature or otherwise—but it was tasty, and I felt it warm my insides almost immediately. It was a better kick than drinking three blood bags at once. Far more successful than a botched middle-school piercing, too.

Collins cleaned up his wrist and applied the bandage. It was less obvious than the holes I'd left in Vin's neck. I offered him a high-five once he'd finished.

"And no tingling in my nethers," he happily proclaimed. "What do you think?"

I nodded and gave him a hopeful grin. "I think I'll put in a good word with Roman tonight."

I didn't expect Vin to be so butt hurt over me drinking Collins' blood, but I got an earful after everyone had left. He sat on my bed as I got dressed in the closet, presenting his argument in a pitifully disappointed tone.

"I like Collins, and I think he's a great addition," he said in a voice that suggested anything but. "I just think it would have been nice if you'd discussed it with me before drinking another man's…fluids."

"Ugh." I poked my head out of the closet to glare at him. "Really? You had to put it that way?"

"Am I wrong?" He pushed his glasses up his nose and folded his arms.

"He bled into a cup. I didn't even touch him."

"That's not the point—"

"Then what *is* the point?" I snapped. "I don't demand that you ask my permission every time you eat, do I?"

"That's different. I'm not eating people," he shouted as I ducked back into the closet to find my cork-heeled sandals. They were the only shoes that would go with the white dress.

"You make me sound like a monster."

"You're not a monster." He groaned. "I'd just like you to be more open and talk with me about these things before you do them. Is that really so much to ask?"

"You can't be my only blood source. That's stupid to even suggest. And I don't see why you think you should be able to dictate to me who else I feed from. That's a little controlling for my tastes, Vin."

I stepped out of the closet to look at myself in the full-length mirror on the back of my door and fingered my hair back into place. I didn't have Vanessa's fancy styling skills, but I'd done a fair job of curling my ends. In the white dress, I looked fit for church. Just so long as no one looked up my skirt and spotted the thigh holster with the .380 Vanessa hadn't asked me to return.

"*That's* what you're wearing tonight?" Vin ogled my reflection from his perch on the bed.

"Are you going to try and tell me that you should have control over my wardrobe now, too?"

"No." His face flushed at the suggestion, which told me well enough that he'd like to. "I just expected you to be in something…black, maybe? You look like you're going to Sunday brunch."

I tilted my head to one side, unable to disagree with him. "I let Mandy pick it out."

Vin's eyebrows rose, and he blinked stiffly. He opened his mouth, but the doorbell cut him off. Same as before, Roman was half an hour early. This time, I was prepared for him, though I did intend to ask what the deal was with the off scheduling.

"Don't wait up." I gave Vin a peck on the cheek and hurried out of my bedroom. He followed, which was unfortunate but not surprising.

"You said he wouldn't be here until eleven."

"That's what I thought," I said with a dismissive shrug.

"But we're not done talking." Vin pushed ahead to cut me off in the mouth of the hallway. "Doesn't this matter to you? Don't *we* matter to you?"

"Vin." I sighed and pressed my lips together. "You knew I had to work tonight—"

"Work?" He scoffed. "They haven't even told you what you're getting paid."

"I'll find out tonight," I said through clenched teeth as the doorbell rang again. "Now, move."

Vin narrowed his eyes, but he pulled his hand off the wall and stepped out of my path. He followed me the rest of the way to the front door, keeping a safe distance behind.

Roman waited on the front porch in a charcoal-gray suit. His jacket was unbuttoned, revealing a crisp, white dress shirt. The look was almost too formal, only being saved by the fact that he wasn't wearing a tie. With his cool blue eyes and tanned skin, he was a sight to behold. A modern-day Apollo. He took in my dress with a subtle glance and then gave me a short nod as if to say it would do. So much for wowing him.

As I stepped out onto the porch, Vin caught the door behind me. "Get her home before sunrise this time," he said, shooting Roman a reprimanding scowl that filled my face with fire.

"Of course." Roman gave me a questioning look, but he didn't say anything until we were closed up in his SUV and heading down the street. "Was there a problem after I dropped you off Tuesday morning?"

"No. Well—" I sighed and rubbed my forehead with one

hand. "It was nothing, really. Vin's just pissy because I drank someone else's blood tonight." I could feel Roman's eyes on me without having to look at him.

"The werewolf girl?" he asked, surprising me with his watered-down language.

"No, actually. The officer you spoke to Monday morning."

"At your house?" He sounded alarmed. "Was this a willing meal?"

"More than willing. He volunteered." I wanted to be offended, but I understood why he would ask. I was a sireless vampling, and he'd caught me red-handed—or red-mouthed, rather—once before.

"That's two for your harem. It's a good start," Roman said.

I nodded, deciding not to share Mandy's offer with him just yet. I still wasn't sure whether or not I would accept it. Besides, I had too much else I wanted to badger him about before we arrived at this party.

"How do most vampires go about building their harems if we're supposed to be so secretive and not tell anyone?"

To my surprise, Roman didn't sigh or grumble at my question. "Most of them have sires with established harems," he said, keeping his eyes on the road as he filled me in. "There are some humans who are freelance donors, like those you saw at the club, but they comprise a minuscule percentage of the population. The rest of the humans who are privy to the supernatural underworld are introduced by sires who either knew them during their mortal years or who took a liking to them after the fact. It's a delicate situation, but most vampires do not have to worry themselves with those details for several decades. You'll need to be very selective about those you add to your harem. If they become a problem, it will be your responsibility to silence them, one way or another, or you'll be held accountable for their actions."

"That's comforting." I rolled my eyes.

"That's valuable information you need to know," he countered. "Here's some more valuable information you might enjoy. The ashes of Pablo Zajalvo, a Spanish vampire who immigrated to the States a decade back, were found in a cabin near Springfield. The reports show that a tornado ripped the roof off, exposing his sleeping body to the sun."

"Ouch." I hissed my sympathy and scowled at Roman. "Why would I enjoy knowing that?"

"Because he received permission to create a scion last year, but he never registered one."

My breath rushed out with trembling anticipation. "Does that mean...?"

"You should read up on the history of his village in Spain, just in case anyone gets nosy and wants to press you for personal details," Roman said. "There's a registration form for you to complete in the glove compartment, and I have a trusted friend willing to write a witness account to prove you're Pablo's scion so the paperwork goes through post-post-mortem."

I swallowed the lump in my throat and refrained from blubbering. "Thank you."

Roman nodded, but his jaw tensed. "It's the least I could do after nearly getting you killed Monday night."

"You didn't—"

"And you should be getting a check in the mail within two weeks. Eight thousand is the high-end for civilian operations, and that's what I put down on the bid sheet I turned in."

"I still want an interview," I injected, hating how ungrateful it made me sound. But everything he was saying had the undertone of dismissal, as if he were trying to pacify me before imparting some massive letdown. "And Collins and Mandy both want interviews, too."

That one did produce a grumble from Roman. "Mandy is too young, without a pack, and she has a record. Your officer friend's chances are only slightly better, but fake sire or not, you're still a scion of House Lilith, and if that information ever comes to light, not only will you be executed, but anyone you've sired will go down with you."

"He doesn't want to be sired," I said, ignoring the chill

that vibrated up my spine. "He just wants a job. He lost his defending my honor."

Roman chuckled. "You seem to inspire that in quite a few men. I've nearly lost my job over you twice now."

The confession sent another chill through my body, and I couldn't help but crack a small smile. "Does that mean you'll help me—help us get in with Blood Vice?"

He shook his head, but the gesture was more in defeat than refusal. "First, let's take care of your sire cover. Then I'll see what I can do."

"Catching this serial killer should help, too, right?"

Roman's brow creased, but he reached across my lap and opened the glovebox, coming away with a manila folder. "I don't think this party is public enough to attract the killer's attention, but just in case."

I flipped the file open and glanced through a small stack of grainy photographs that looked as if they'd been taken from the club video footage. I spotted the most recent victim in the last shot, his back turned to the camera. I wouldn't have known it was him if not for the red circle drawn around his head. A dark-haired woman in a black gown stood at his side. I could only see her profile, but she could have easily been one of the Elviras I'd encountered in the back hallway.

"This is it?" I asked.

Roman nodded. "And since the body wasn't found on

club property, and we obtained the video footage without a warrant, we weren't allowed to shut the place down and search for more evidence."

"So, just as much red tape bullshit as the human authorities deal with. Check."

Roman's hands gripped the steering wheel tighter as he turned off Ladue Road and into one of the fancy neighborhoods just past the Country Club golf course. A few minutes later, we pulled into an extra-wide driveway lined with luxury cars on either side.

We found a parking spot, and Roman killed the SUV's engine. "I wouldn't mention Zajalvo to anyone for now," he said. "The news of his death hasn't been publicly shared since there's an open investigation."

"Okay," I whispered breathlessly as I took in the looming house. The impressive landscaping was lit up with park quality lanterns that rendered the entire front lawn bright as day. "What *should* I talk about with these people? What could I possibly have in common with them?" I asked, eyeing their fancy cars.

Mandy had been right. The few vampires I spotted making their way down the paved drive were in black cocktail dresses. They were classier than the clubgoers, but they still exuded Vanessa's brand of tasteful goth.

"One of the instructors from the training center is

supposed to be here tonight," Roman said. "I'll introduce you to him, and maybe he'll have better luck talking you out of this nonsense."

"Training center? You mean like Quantico?"

"Blood Vice has their own facility in Denver. If you get this interview you want so badly, the training program will be your next hurdle."

"How long does training take? Are there different programs for half-sireds and werewolves?"

Roman held up a hand to quiet me. "Why don't you save your questions for the expert?" He exited the SUV before I could argue and circled around to my side as I opened my door, offering his hand to help me out of the vehicle.

"Thanks," I said under my breath, feeling a little foolish for my nerves and eagerness to know all the things at once. I needed to do some breathing exercises or something if I didn't want to scare this new source of intel off.

Roman gave my hand a squeeze before letting it go. "I like the dress," he said softly as if he knew I needed the reassurance. What I didn't need were any more butterflies in my stomach.

"I like your suit," I said, returning his compliment with an appreciative glance.

He grinned. "Let's go rub some elbows."

"And maybe catch a serial killer."

Roman snorted. "Who says I don't know how to show a girl a good time?"

# Chapter Eighteen

Ladue was where all the doctors and lawyers flocked to in St. Louis. The houses were huge with ample lawns and swimming pools. If Laura hadn't run off to be a star, I could picture her somewhere like this, maybe as a trophy wife raising a brood of spoiled children. I'd probably get a Christmas card every year that looked like a Ralph Lauren ad.

The house where the party was taking place was a brick two-story with tall, arched windows and dark shutters. Silhouettes moved around behind gauzy curtains, and I wondered if the duke's emissary—this friend of Vanessa's— was human. Or maybe he slept in the basement. Perhaps there were internal shutters that sealed the place up tight. I had more questions than I knew what to do with.

"Didn't you say that the duke has a mansion around here?" I whispered to Roman as we headed up the long drive toward the front entrance.

"His estate is half a mile west of here." He dipped his head down close to my ear as we neared the door, and I caught the scent of his cologne, a smoky blend of patchouli and new leather. "Don't forget that there will be a lot of older vampires here tonight, and many of them have exceptional hearing."

I nodded, silently vowing to zip my lips as he rang the doorbell. The paneled door matched the shutters, and as it slid open, light spilled out to greet us, along with a tall woman in a burgundy sheath dress. Her strawberry locks lay over one shoulder, and sharp, blue eyes twinkled as she touched Roman's shoulder familiarly.

"Roman! Nigel will be so glad you made it." Her friendly smile turned to me next. "And he will absolutely want to meet your date. I'm Sara. It's lovely to meet you." She held her hand out, and I grasped it reflexively, taking note of the warmth of her skin and the steady thrum of her pulse. *Human.*

"I'm Jenna," I said when her eyebrows lifted expectantly. Social cues weren't something I was good at as a human, and that clearly hadn't improved after my death.

"There's a table of hors d'oeuvres in the dining room for the daywalkers," Sara said as she led us through the foyer. "And Nigel flew in the Blood House Geishas for the evening if you're hungry, Jenna," she added, glancing over her shoulder at me.

I saw Roman's jaw flex from the corner of my eye and offered Sara a polite smile. "I've already eaten, but thank you."

She cocked her head as if surprised that I would refuse such an offer. "Suit yourself."

The foyer opened into a large room with vaulted ceilings and a massive fireplace. The light hardwood floors and pale walls made the space seem even bigger. A man and woman rested on a leather sofa, and another couple stood in a doorway that looked as if it led into a kitchen. They spared us a cordial glance as we joined them.

The wall of windows that spanned the backside of the house was bare, giving a glowing view of the outside patio and the swimming pool beyond. Flower-shaped lanterns floated across the water. Guests congregated around pub tables that lined the balcony railing of the patio. I spotted a few small plates filled with finger foods and several tiny goblets of what looked to be dark wine.

It was hard to tell what the ratio of humans to vampires might be since there were no color-coded bracelets to go by. Not that it really mattered tonight. I was well fed, and everyone here was obviously in the know. It was an attractive crowd, and they were all tastefully dressed. Aside from the alabaster skin most of them possessed that seemed out of place in the heart of summer, they appeared perfectly normal.

"I'll let Nigel know you've arrived," Sara said, making her way toward a staircase tucked against the interior wall. "Make yourselves at home."

Roman brushed back the folds of his jacket and tucked his hands into the pockets of his dress pants. "You can sample the Geishas if you'd like, though they serve by tap only." He nodded at an abandoned glass on the sideboard table near the stairs.

I wanted to ask if that really made such a difference, but

I was afraid someone might overhear my neophyte question. I would have a hard enough time making conversation without exposing my vampling status, so I filed it away under things I'd pester Roman about on the ride home.

"What's so special about this geisha blood?" I asked instead.

"For one, it's organic." Roman paused and rolled his shoulders. "But a lot of the elite harems are, so that's not so special in this circle. The Blood House Geishas follow rigorous diets that flavor their blood." *Intriguing.*

"Flavor it like what?"

Roman opened his mouth but then paused as if unsure how to answer.

"Like sex on Sunday morning," a deep voice boomed.

My shoulders bunched, and I twisted around in time with Roman to find a mammoth of a man standing behind us in the opening of the foyer. His smooth head nearly grazed the arched passageway as he stepped inside the room with us, but it wasn't until I saw him side by side with Roman that I truly grasped how tall he was.

I couldn't peg his race, but he wasn't Caucasian, which, with his ashen skin tone, alerted me to the fact that he was a vampire. Of course, his comment about the geisha blood had tipped me off first. A midnight-blue suit hugged his Goliath frame, pairing nicely with a baby-blue dress shirt and a matching pocket square.

"What's happening, Ghostfang?" he said to Roman, reaching out to clasp hands with him before engaging in some dude-bro half-hug.

"Ghostfang?" I blinked at Roman, enjoying the way the tips of his ears reddened.

"A nickname he picked up at the bat cave," the man answered for him. Then he held his hand out to me. "Well, hello there. I'm Kai." I let him take my hand, but instead of the awkward gesture he'd performed with Roman, he turned it over and laid a soft kiss on my knuckles.

"Jenna, this is Kai Natani, the instructor from the training center I was telling you about." Roman cleared his throat and scratched the back of his head. I couldn't decide if he was more uncomfortable about me seeing him interact so casually with another vampire or about the way that vampire was interacting with me.

"It's so nice to meet you," I said, giving Kai what I hoped was a flirty smile. "I'd love to learn more about the training program."

"Jenna's thinking about applying for Blood Vice," Roman added.

"Really?" Kai gave me a once-over. "A sweet thing like you?"

I did my best to ignore his patronizing tone and kept my

smile in place. "I was a police officer as a human, and I enjoyed the line of work."

He laughed. "Blood Vice is quite a leap."

"How so?"

"I'll leave you two to it," Roman said, taking the opportunity to excuse himself. "I need to have a quick word with Nigel."

Kai watched him head up the same stairs we'd seen Sara use a few moments before. Once Roman was out of sight, Kai's focus returned to me.

"How long have you been seeing Roman?" he asked, ignoring my earlier question.

"We're just friends," I said, wondering if that were even true. "I helped him with a few cases recently."

"Ah." Kai gave me a knowing grin. "So that's where your interest in Blood Vice stemmed from." Sure, that would work well enough.

"What's the bat cave?"

He bellowed out a hearty laugh. "It's what we call the BATC facility in Denver. Blood Authority Training Center," he added for clarity.

"How long is the program there?"

"Three grueling months."

I shrugged and folded my hands over the skirt of my dress. "That's only half as long as the police academy."

"Trust me," Kai said with an arrogant grin, "it will feel ten-times longer."

I didn't blink. "Where do I sign up?"

He seemed mildly impressed, but I could tell he wasn't taking me seriously. Still, he offered up a dismissive answer. "Have your sire send a recommendation letter to the Duke of House Lilith, and maybe you'll get a callback for an interview."

"I'll do that," I said, remembering Roman's warning about dodging talk of my sire.

"Then maybe I'll see you this fall." Kai's attention strayed over my shoulder, and then he gave me a polite smile. "Excuse me for a moment."

"Of course."

He sidestepped around me, and I turned in time to watch him follow a woman in a teal kimono through a doorway at the opposite end of the room. The beginning of another staircase showed just beyond, and soft music drifted up from below, the slow plucking of strings and a mournful flute.

I considered following him, but that he hadn't invited me along told me he wasn't interested in continuing our conversation. I also felt odd about venturing too far without Roman, though the other guests in the room had all migrated outside or downstairs while I'd been visiting with Kai. Now, I was all alone.

A waiter with a tray of blood-filled glasses cut through the room and headed outside to the patio. When he returned, he stopped to collect an empty glass off the fireplace mantel. He caught sight of me and crossed the room to offer up the last glass of blood on his tray.

"Thank you." I took the glass to be polite, not entirely sure if I'd sample it. The waiter's head snapped up at the sound of my voice, and he stumbled back a step.

"You're the girl from the club," he hissed. "I lost my job because of you."

I sucked in a startled breath and stared at him, suddenly recognizing the bartender from Bleeders. Without the cutoff dress shirt and bowtie, I hadn't recognized him. Nigel and Sara dressed their staff in more tasteful, traditional attire. The man continued to glare at me, but I certainly wasn't about to apologize.

"Better than losing your head," I quipped.

"Is there a problem?" Sara asked as she descended the open staircase.

"No, ma'am." The waiter bowed and hurried off to the kitchen.

Sara tsked. "New help. They take a while to break in."

I nodded as if I had any idea what she was talking about.

"What do you think?" she asked, glancing down at my untested glass.

I swirled the blood a moment and then finally decided to brave a small taste. Sara watched me closely, but I dismissed her the second the blood hit my tongue. Color exploded behind my eyes, a kaleidoscope of crystalline hues that danced in time with the flavors coating my palate. The sweet, fruity tang had an herbal aftertaste, and when the glass ran empty, I almost cried.

Like a savage, I shook the glass over my open mouth, longing for just one more drop. My eyes refocused on the room, and then on Sara's appalled expression. I snapped my lips shut as heat ravaged my face and neck. And then that last drop I'd hoped to savor dripped onto the front of my dress.

Sara cleared her throat and pointed a finger above her own breast. "You got a little… There's some hydrogen peroxide and salt water spray under the sink in the guest bath," she said, then nodded toward a small door tucked under the staircase.

"Thanks," I whispered, my voice barely able to rise above my sinking dignity.

I hurried past her and ducked into the bathroom. There was just enough room for me to stand between the toilet and the sink vanity. Maybe if I prayed hard enough, the door would vanish, and I could die in here.

The geisha blood felt heavy on the back of my tongue. First, I'd wanted more. Now, I never wanted it again. I was so stupid. How could I have let this happen? What was Roman thinking, bringing me to this party? I was an embarrassment to vampires everywhere. He should have done the right thing and put me out of my misery months ago.

As tears filled my eyes, I tried to blink them away so I could see to fix the stain setting into my dress. I found the bottle of peroxide under the sink and tore the hand towel off the hook to dab at the ugly spot.

My anger shifted to Mandy next, for picking out the dress in the first place, and then to my sister for leaving me no other choice but to infiltrate this strange new world of failure and humiliation. A sob slipped from me as I worked the stain with little result. Then a soft knock at the door made me jump.

"Jenna?" Roman whispered. "It's just me." I reached for the lock, but he twisted the knob before I could latch it and slipped inside the tiny room with me. I pressed my back against the floral wallpaper, but that still only left a few inches between us. In the mirror above the sink, we looked cozy enough to be a wedding cake topper.

"What happened?" Roman asked.

"I'm an idiot." I covered my face and took a shuddering sob. "I tried the fancy fucking blood and made a complete ass out of myself—and I ruined my dress in the process."

"Let me see." Roman's warm fingers coiled around my wrists, and he gently pried my hands away from my face and chest, revealing the dime-sized splotch to the left side of my chest, just a few inches below my collarbone. "It's not so bad."

"Then why am I a train wreck right now?" I asked.

"Because geisha blood amplifies everything you're feeling." He gave me a pointed look. "So I'm guessing you were a bundle of nerves. Understandable. Don't beat yourself up over it."

"You should have seen Sara's face," I whispered.

Fresh mortification tore through me, but Roman fended it off by tugging the towel out of my hand. He picked up the peroxide from the counter and splashed it directly onto my dress, giving it only a split second to bubble before he dabbed me with the towel. His brows knit together as he focused on my chest, leaning in to get a closer look at the fabric, and then a different brand of humiliation overpowered me.

"There," he finally said, leaning back so I could take a look. All that remained was a wet spot. "All better."

"No, it's not." I looked up at him through my lashes. "I don't know what I'm doing. I don't know how to be a vampire."

Roman sighed and reached out to tuck my hair behind one ear. His fingers trailed down the side of my neck and came to rest on my shoulder. We were so close, I could see my pitiful reflection in his blue eyes.

"It will get easier. It takes time." He gave me a sad smile. "And in this world, time is all we have."

The worst of the geisha blood was starting to wear off, but my foolish shame lingered. "I know you need to stay for this party, but I just can't. I'm going to call a cab."

Roman shook his head. "I'll drive you home. Vanessa will understand."

"Or she'll hate me even more than she already does," I grumbled.

"She doesn't hate you. The club assignment is ancient history."

I snorted. "Your girlfriend doesn't seem like the forgiving kind."

"She's not my girlfriend." Roman's eyes fell away from mine, and he reached up to tuck my hair back again. When his fingers began to slip away from my face, I cupped my hand around his and pressed my cheek into his palm. "Jenna, I—"

The bathroom door whipped open, smacking against the exterior wall. Roman ripped away from me to turn around. Over his shoulder, I spied the bartender from the club. The man's face was blank, no trace of the irritation I'd seen when he offered me the glass of blood. A long, slender knife was gripped in one hand, and he thrust it into the room.

Roman's elbow connected with my sternum as he deflected the first blow. The blade gouged the wall beside me with a dull thud. When it withdrew, Roman hissed. The sleeve of his gray suit darkened with blood. He reached inside the fold of his jacket, likely for his gun, but the bartender's blade was too fast. It sliced through Roman's arm and into his chest, skewering his limb in place. The tip of the knife poked through his back between his shoulder blades, tenting the material of his jacket before slicing clean through.

I screamed.

And then I filled the bartender's face full of Silver Wolfsbane. I didn't remember pulling the gun out of my thigh holster, and it didn't register that it was in my hand until the magazine clicked empty. The man staggered backward, extracting the knife from Roman as he fell dead to the floor. His face was no longer recognizable, just a shredded puddle of meat.

Roman wasn't much better off. He gurgled and dropped to his knees, blocking the doorway of the bathroom. I stumbled over his legs and knelt down beside him, grasping his shoulders as he toppled over onto his back.

"No, no, no." I ripped open Roman's dress shirt and pressed my hands over the hole in his chest, but I couldn't apply enough pressure to stop the river of blood leaking out of him. It oozed up between my fingers and spread in a puddle across the hardwood, soaking into the hem of my dress and the white hair at the nape of Roman's neck. More bubbled up from his gaping mouth as his panicked eyes sought mine.

"I don't know what to do," I sobbed. "Oh God, what do I do?"

I couldn't think straight. There was too much blood everywhere, and nothing made sense. Something instinctual triggered in my brain, and the next thing I knew, I was biting down on my own wrist, tearing at the flesh with my fangs.

Dark blood swelled up from beneath my skin, and I held it over Roman's mouth, flexing my fingers to encourage more to come. This had to work. It had worked for me.

My blood trickled into Roman's mouth, mixing with his. His throat bobbed, swallowing reflexively. He closed his eyes and groaned something unintelligible against my wrist before latching on and sucking hard.

Under the wave of relief, a bittersweet tinge of arousal stirred. It floated in the background, subdued by the immediate danger Roman was in—and suppressed even further by the guests who had finally located us, thanks to the shots I'd fired.

"The hell was that?" The growing crowd parted, and Kai emerged with a hulking pistol gripped in one hand. Sara wasn't far behind him.

"What have you done?" she shrieked at me.

Roman still drank from my wrist, and my breath had grown too shallow to muster up a reply. I glanced across the room to where the bartender's dead body lay beside the bloody knife. My hand over Roman's chest painted the rest of the story.

A few minutes later, he exhaled a breath that didn't produce more blood and was able to sit up and confirm what had happened. Between the blade and the club connection, it was quickly assessed that we'd found our serial killer. Bartending at Bleeders had clearly helped facilitate the murders. By getting the creep fired, I'd dubbed myself his next target. I played bait far better than I realized.

I should have been happy. I *wanted* to be happy. But the way Roman refused to look at me told me something wasn't quite right, and I felt too drained, literally and emotionally, to celebrate.

Kai praised my fast thinking and offered to put in a good word with the duke. And Sara apologized for her accusing outburst, though, I declined when she offered me more geisha blood. I'd had enough mood swings for one night to last a lifetime.

No one bothered to ask Roman what we were doing in the bathroom together. So I didn't either.

# Chapter Nineteen

The ride home was chilly. Mostly because Roman had the air conditioner cranked up to an artic setting I assumed was another fancy upgrade included in the SUV's police package. The tank top and shorts Sara had loaned me didn't help.

Roman was in a pair of jogging shorts and a tee shirt borrowed from Nigel. We'd both showered at the manor before leaving, and our ruined party clothes had been tossed. Peroxide wasn't going to cut it this time.

When we pulled into my driveway, Roman didn't kill the SUV's engine. He was still avoiding looking at me, too. I hadn't asked why, but I had a feeling he was getting ready to let me know. The anticipation coiled my guts up like a jack-in-the-box.

Roman's hands gripped the leather steering wheel until his knuckles turned white. Then he cleared his throat.

"Do you remember what I told you would happen to anyone you sired?" he said.

I hugged myself and shivered. "That they would die with me if the truth about my sire was ever discovered."

"Yes. That." Roman nodded stiffly. "If I had died tonight, you would have been considered my sire, because your blood would have been freshest in my system. Do you understand that?"

My lungs grew heavy as I blinked at him. "What are you saying? That I should have let you die?"

"That is *exactly* what I am saying." Roman's jaw flexed, and he finally looked at me. Anger glazed his eyes. "I would have risen as Vanessa's scion, and I would have been pardoned the remaining fifty years of my contract for dying in the line of duty."

I covered my mouth with my hand. Hot tears spilled over my knuckles. "I'm so sorry, Roman. I didn't know what else to do. I was afraid, and there was so much blood. I didn't want you to die because of me."

He sighed and turned to gaze out the windshield. "At least you got the killer. That will look good on your résumé, won't it?" His sarcasm stabbed at my heart, and it was a struggle to inhale my next breath.

"I'm sorry," I choked out again. "I wasn't trying to get anyone. I just wanted to save you, the same way you saved me. I didn't mean to—"

"I know," he cut me off. "I know, okay. You were only trying to help."

"I'm sorry."

"You can stop apologizing." Roman looked down at his lap. "I need to find Vanessa before sunrise. If I were to somehow die before she anoints me again…that would not be good. And you need to feed anyway," he added, dismissing me.

I climbed out of the SUV and hurried up the front walk without looking back. Roman pulled out of the driveway and was halfway down my block before I reached the front porch. I slipped inside and felt my way through the dark, closing myself inside my bedroom before launching into a complete meltdown.

I don't know what I had expected after saving his life, but it wasn't this. If I hadn't felt like a hero before, I certainly didn't feel like one now. I wasn't even the villain in this story. I was the pathetic catalyst that screwed everything up and expected everyone else to somehow fix it.

I expected Laura to stay and play my daytime counterpart. I expected Vin to give me blood and not request a serious commitment in return. I expected Roman to help me land a job I didn't deserve and wasn't qualified for. There was also the shameful expectation I secretly harbored. I *wanted* Roman—his heart, body, and blood—despite the fact that he was sworn to someone else, however platonic he made out their relationship to be.

I was hungry, but my insides ached too much to eat. After geisha blood, the bagged variety was practically dog vomit. And after experiencing Roman's gentle side, his wrath was a cyclone of razorblades. Why did my whole life feel like one step forward and ten steps back lately?

It was still a few hours until sunrise, but I curled up in the fetal position on my bed, willing the night to be over. Wretched thoughts burned through my brain. Maybe it was time to give up. Maybe I should rip the curtains from my bedroom walls so the sun would burn me alive. Maybe everyone would be better off that way.

The thought was fleeting. I wasn't suicidal—just wallowing in self-pity—but as if my dark thoughts had decided to manifest on their own, the plaid curtains over my bedroom window billowed inward. Thin moonlight spilled across the wall, and a silhouette crept through it.

A silhouette wielding a long blade.

# Chapter Twenty

My heart stuttered out a nervous rhythm. There was no way that bartender had survived what I'd done to his face. Which could only mean there was more than one killer. Just what I needed tonight.

My sluggish brain struggled to come up with a plan as my blood vision kicked in, lighting up the room in shades of crimson. I slid off the far side of the bed and soundlessly opened the top drawer of my nightstand, clenching my teeth when I remembered that my service pistol had been reclaimed by Langford. My backup Glock was in the drawer of the china cabinet in the dining room.

A hiss sliced through the air, and I recoiled as the newcomer's blade split open the pillows along my headboard. Feathers erupted like confetti, and I stumbled back a step as the killer leapt onto the bed. My blood vision pulsed, and despite the downy rain, I picked out the features of an Elvira lookalike I'd encountered at Bleeders—high cheekbones, arched brows, blunt bangs. She wore a black bodysuit and matching knee high boots. Very ninja goth.

"For Patrick!" She pointed her blade at my face and charged.

In my retreat, I cracked my shoulder against the bathroom doorframe, and then my opposite hand nearly missed the doorknob as I struggled to open it without taking my eyes from the crazed intruder. My clumsiness cost me dearly.

When the door finally sprang open, I was pushed backward into the bathroom. I fell, landing on my ass. The weight of a boot shoved into my chest, expelling the air from my lungs, and then my head bounced off the tile, causing the nightlight on the wall to multiply across my vision. For a second, I forgot how to make words.

The woman's knife pierced my shoulder and pinned me to the floor. She gripped the handle of the blade with both hands and dragged it inward toward my heart, tearing an inhuman scream from my throat. I tasted bile on my tongue as I sucked in a rasping breath.

My legs thrashed about, kicking open drawers on the vanity. I felt like a squirming insect, seconds away from having my insides splattered across the floor, grasping at anything within reach. My fingers clawed at the shower curtain until it broke loose, bringing the rod down with it, while my opposite hand found the dangling cord of the curling iron. I whipped it off the counter, smacking the hard, plastic handle into the side of the woman's head.

She growled and freed one hand from the knife in order to wrench the curling iron away from me, chucking it over her shoulder. Before her hand made it back to the hilt of her blade, the cord of the curling iron looped around her neck. It dug into her skin, drawing a surprised gasp as she released her hold on the knife.

My red tunnel vision expanded, and Mandy appeared in the threshold of the bathroom in her angry unicorn pajamas. One hand gripped the barrel of the curling iron, and the other tangled in the cord. She shoved her knee into the woman's back and held tight, strangling her for all she was worth.

The tag-team effort allowed just enough time for me to reach a shaky hand up and jerk the blade free of my shoulder. It hurt even worse coming out. Blood spurted across the tile and oozed down into my armpit.

I pulled myself up to a sitting position and glared at the asphyxiating woman standing before me. She hissed as she tried to pry her fingers under the cord around her neck. Then the underside of her boot connected with my jaw, and my face smashed into the vanity, slamming shut one of the drawers I'd kicked open.

"Die, motherfucker!" Mandy screamed, losing her grip on the curling iron. And she'd been doing so well cleaning up her gutter mouth. A little violence, and we were right back to square one.

The woman twisted in her grip. Her knee came up, and in a flash, a second blade slipped out of her boot and into Mandy's stomach. The girl's cry echoed my own.

I shot to my feet, panic and terror serving up a second wind that shook loose every ounce of energy left in my body. I couldn't fail Mandy. She was my responsibility, and I would *not* lose her. Not to this bitch or any other.

I snatched a handful of the woman's hair and yanked. She reeled back as if to deliver a punch, but I caught her arm and dug my fingers into the meat of her biceps. Between my rage and pain and hunger, instinct took over.

My fangs flicked out, and I bit down on the curve of her neck, right where the collar of her spandex suit began. Blood soaked the slick material, and I burrowed my face in deeper, my teeth tearing through the fabric and her flesh until the flow thickened.

The woman twitched and squealed in my arms, sending a blissful thrill of excitement through me. I hadn't fed this enthusiastically since the carjacking incident. The adrenaline and fear were intoxicating—almost better than the arousal when I fed from Vin.

My skin tingled, and something in my core tightened as the woman's blood filled me. The hole in my shoulder itched. It felt like hundreds of squirming maggots were filling the wound, until it sealed up tight, and the disturbing sensation ended, taking my pain along with it.

I expected my thirst to diminish, but it kept building as if leading up to some grand climax. I wanted to suck her dry.

Some part of me knew it would be pure ecstasy. I could *feel* it.

That feeling died when I caught sight of Mandy looking up at me from the bathroom floor, pain and horror twisting up her features.

The woman had lost consciousness at some point, and when I retracted my fangs from her, she crumpled to the tile floor. She wasn't dead yet. I'd felt a sluggish pulse before guilt begged me to stop feeding, but I didn't know how long she would last without medical attention. At this moment, I didn't care. Mandy was my only concern.

The girl's pajama shirt was soaked with blood. It was darkest where the knife had struck her, spreading out from there. She'd already removed the blade, but she was in no hurry to get up. I knelt down beside her.

"Let me see," I demanded when she recoiled. I couldn't tell if the wound or my violent feeding was more to blame for her dilated eyes and shallow breath.

"I need…I need to shift," she rasped. "I'll heal faster that way."

"Is there anything I can do?" I asked, stroking her arm as I eyed the gash in her abdomen.

She pressed her lips together and shook her head. "Just give me some space."

"Freeze!" Laura sprang around the corner, clutching my Glock with both hands. She wore one of her lacy nighties, and her newly red hair was pinned up in foam curlers. Her breath sounded as if she'd run around the house a dozen times before finding her way here. Wide, blue eyes darted from me to the unconscious murderess to Mandy. "Oh my God! I'll call an ambulance!"

"No!" Mandy and I both shouted.

"Right! Right. Shit." Laura bounced on the balls of her feet, then her eyes fell on the woman again. "Is that the serial killer? In our freaking house?"

I grimaced. "One of them."

"Oh, that's just perfect." Laura huffed out a trembling breath. "Who are we supposed to call? Is there a number for this?"

"I need to shift, like now," Mandy said. Her teeth chattered, and her lips had taken on a blue tint.

I stood and edged around her to get out of the bathroom, encouraging Laura back as I went. I held my hand out for the gun, and she turned it over with an anxious frown.

"I can't believe I was ready to shoot someone. Oh my God. I'm shaking." She fluttered her pink-tipped fingernails and shivered.

"House of the brave, right here," I said, shooting a nervous glance over my shoulder to where Mandy had begun her transformation. Laura noticed, too. She paled and inched toward my bedroom door.

"I'll just go make us some coffee," she said, then added, "You'd better call blondie to come clean this up."

My stomach roiled at the thought of reaching out to Roman again so soon, but there was really no other choice. It wasn't like I had a number for anyone else in Blood Vice—in the vampire community, period. I needed to fix that. Soon. For all I knew, Roman wouldn't even answer my call.

I crossed my room and pushed back the bedroom curtains to investigate how the killer had gained access. A perfect circle of glass had been cut from one window pane. It was just wide enough for someone to slip their hand through to unlock the latch. I stared out the window, glancing up and down the street to see if there were any unfamiliar vehicles parked nearby. Then I quit stalling and dialed Roman's number.

He answered on the first ring.

"Are you okay?" His voice rushed out in a panicked breath. I could hear the roar of an engine humming in the background.

"I am now," I said, relief flooding through me so suddenly that it brought tears to my eyes. "Mandy will be after she shifts. But the woman who broke into my house to kill me might not last long with the degree of blood loss she's suffered. If you want to question her, you better get here fast."

"I'm almost there," Roman said.

My heart ached, painting a warped fantasy of him rushing back to apologize for words he didn't mean. To take me in his arms and press his lips to mine. I held my breath, waiting for the truth before I humiliated myself more than I already had.

"You fed me…a lot of blood." Roman struggled to get the words out. "There are certain side effects. I'm compelled to come to your aid until Vanessa sets things straight."

"Oh." I swallowed, dying a little as my delusion dissipated. "I didn't know. I'm sorry."

"Don't—" Roman sighed. "I'm going to call Vanessa in since she's taking point on this case. We'll be there shortly."

He ended the call without saying goodbye.

With everything that had happened tonight, I hadn't considered Vanessa. The idea of facing her after I'd practically poached her potential scion sent my recently replenished pulse into overdrive. Getting into a catfight with a femme fatal vampire over a simple misunderstanding wasn't how I wanted to end my night.

Seeing how the culprit was unconscious in my bathroom, I didn't think it was necessary to leave the crime scene untouched for evidence. So while Laura fixed coffee and Mandy licked the blood from her fur, I sealed up the window with a piece of cardboard and some packing tape.

Then I stripped out of Sara's destroyed loaner clothes and into a fresh pair of jeans and a tank top. I took a damp wash cloth to my face and neck, scrubbing where blood had dried to my skin. Most of it wiped away without too much effort, but my hair would have to wait until I had a chance to take a shower.

Emotionally, I felt drained and ragged. But it didn't show. I'd fed—long and hard—and my skin glowed with a dewy etherealness that made me less self-conscious about the dried gore in my hair. It also took the edge off my raw nerves as I awaited Roman and Vanessa's arrival.

An unmarked Charger pulled up to the curb first. Vanessa exited the driver's side. She wore her usual black tactical gear, and I wondered if she'd been working another assignment tonight. Maybe that was why she hadn't been able to attend the party. To my surprise, Kai Natani opened the passenger's door. He was still in his flashy blue suit.

A second later, Roman's SUV parked behind them. It was as if he had intentionally waited for Vanessa to arrive first. I didn't blame him. Explaining what had happened was going to make her question his loyalties enough as it was. From Nigel's borrowed clothes, I was guessing he hadn't made it home before turning around. Vanessa frowned at him, but she didn't comment.

"Two in one night," Kai said as he stepped up onto my front porch. He had to duck to clear the roof overhang. "You're my kinda girl." He gave me an obnoxious grin that I couldn't bring myself to return.

"She's in here," I said, turning to lead him through the front door without greeting Vanessa or Roman. I didn't know what to say to either of them.

Mandy had shifted back to her human form and put on a fresh pair of pajamas. She and Laura sat at the kitchen table, sipping sugared up mugs of coffee and talking in hushed voices. The extra blood in my system boosted my senses, and I overheard bits and pieces of what they were saying.

I pushed their conversation to the back of my mind, determined to stay focused. I would handle my damaged home life later. After the big, bad vamps hauled off the serial killer dozing in my bathroom.

Kai lifted an eyebrow as he took in the feathers littering my bedroom floor. Then he sniffed the air. The bitter odor of stale blood was strong—probably potent enough that an average human could detect it.

Kai followed his nose toward the bathroom. I stepped back and folded my arms, letting him go ahead of me. Vanessa and Roman were right behind him, taking in the damage to my home with dispassionate eyes.

"She came through the window," I said, pointing across

the room. "My partner, Mandy Starsgard, helped incapacitate her. I'd probably be dead if she hadn't intervened."

Roman's eyes locked on mine. His jaw flexed, and he swallowed.

"Do you recognize her?" Vanessa asked, giving her back to Roman as she stepped into the bathroom and knelt down.

"Yeah." I nodded and rubbed a hand up the back of one arm. "She was at Bleeders Monday night. She's the one who was last seen with the victim in the dumpster."

Kai pressed his fingers to the side of the woman's throat—the side I hadn't mauled. "I think she'll live." He peeled her collar back and took a closer look at a tiny, faint, circular scar. My breath caught, and a burning sensation pinched along my neck.

Kai lifted an eyebrow. "Looks like she might have a potential sire who has some explaining to do."

"Let me see that." Vanessa pulled a small flashlight from her pocket and centered it over the scar. She pressed a button, and the light changed to green and then blue. A flash sounded, and I added the fancy gadget to my Christmas wish list.

Vanessa stood and gave Roman a worried look that slowly transferred to his own expression, while Kai heaved the woman up over his shoulder, letting her arms and head dangle down his backside. I cringed, thinking of the stains he'd find on his fancy suit later, but he didn't seem bothered.

He turned to glance in the blood-spattered mirror above my sink and ran a hand over his bald head as if fixing an invisible mop of hair.

"All set?" he asked.

Vanessa's phone rang before she had a chance to reply, and a crease formed across her brow as she answered the call. "Your Grace?"

Roman glanced at me again, but I couldn't read his expression. If he wasn't bouncing between irrational jealousy and guilt-ridden atonement, his mood toward me often seemed to settle on annoyed indifference. After the events of the night, I wasn't sure where that left us.

"We've just collected a second suspect, one that's still breathing," Vanessa said into her phone. I didn't have to guess to know she was referring to the lead sandwich I'd fed the bartender. "The same vampire who eliminated the first suspect. She's a civilian contact of Roman Knight's, sir." Vanessa shot me a look as unreadable as Roman's. "Her name is Jenna Skye. Of course, sir. Straightaway."

"What's the word?" Kai asked, readjusting the woman on his shoulder.

Vanessa licked the corner of her mouth and blinked stiffly. "He wants to see us in his office. Now."

"Then let's go," Kai said.

"*All* of us." Vanessa's eyes landed on me again. If I hadn't been so terrified of her, I'd say she was feeling sorry for me. "That includes you," she said.

"Are you sure?" Roman's eyes dilated, panic reducing his blue irises to thin, ghostly rings.

Vanessa ignored his question and led us out of my bedroom and down the hallway. Kai and Roman followed with me trailing behind. The light in the kitchen was still on, but Laura and Mandy had disappeared, probably to take Duncan out back.

"She'll ride with you," Vanessa said to Roman. "You can fill her in on the proper etiquette for addressing the duke."

"Can't you do that?" Roman balked as she reached the front door and held it open for Kai to carry the woman through.

Vanessa's piercing, green eyes took Roman in with wrathful skepticism. My heart dropped when her attention snapped to me. Could she tell what I'd done just by looking at us? I bit my tongue, refraining from hurling a premature apology at her, and suffered through the discomfort until she turned back to Roman.

"This is your mess. I told you that from day one. Fix it, or I will." She turned and followed Kai outside. The door slammed behind her, and Roman loosed a shuddering breath. He ran a hand over his face, pausing to press his thumb and forefinger into his closed eyelids.

"This is not good," he groaned. *Wasn't it?*

This was what I'd been asking for. An audience with this duke was what I needed if I wanted to join Blood Vice. But the way Vanessa, an experienced, tough-as-coffin-nails vampire, reacted to this man sent up red flags galore. My excitement was also stunted by the unintentional suffering I'd caused Roman, especially after he'd stuck his neck out so far to help me—finding a sire I could claim and introducing me to the elite of the vampire community.

"We need to get going," Roman said. "The duke doesn't appreciate waiting."

"Should I change?" I asked, glancing down at my tank top and jeans, and then at his sweats. "Should *you* change?"

"No time." Roman pushed open the front door and waited for me to exit ahead of him. "I still have to cover the basics with you before we get there, and it's a short drive."

"I don't know. Maybe this isn't such a great idea." I glanced behind me, searching for my sister and Mandy. "I mean, I haven't even filled out the registration paperwork for that Spanish sire you found."

Roman's face flushed, and he ground his teeth. "Keep your voice down," he hissed. "Your pet mutt will hear, and I already told you I won't admit to any involvement."

"Fine, but the point still stands. What if I'm asked about my sire?"

He shook his head. "Doesn't matter now. The duke has demanded your presence. The decision is out of your hands. Mine, too."

"*Demanded* my presence?" I folded my arms. The finality of his statement grated on me, and I considered refusing. But Roman's face hardened when I didn't move.

"I don't want to do this the hard way," he said. "But I'm not losing my job over you. Not tonight. Let's go."

Guilt slithered around my heart and squeezed.

"I appreciate everything you've done for me." I released my arms down to my sides and sighed. "And I really am sorry for the trouble I've caused you."

Roman frowned, and I could tell he was wallowing in his own guilt. "Water under the bridge." Then he pushed the door open farther and narrowed his eyes at me. "I won't ask again."

# Chapter Twenty-one

The duke's manor was situated in a more secluded nook in Ladue. Several acres of well-groomed woods surrounded the stone and glass fortress. It was easily three times as large as Nigel's place down the road.

I wanted to ask Roman what was up with all these fancy vampires and their obsession with enormous windows. Was it a way of flaunting their fearlessness? Or was it an added element to disguise their true nature? I bit my tongue, deciding to save the question for someone who wasn't actively loathing me.

"Repeat it back so I know you were listening," Roman said as the SUV slowed and turned down the driveway.

"Don't speak unless spoken to. Keep my eyes on the floor. Bow at the neck, and address him as Your Grace," I parroted back to him.

"And if he asks, which he will likely do, your sire left without specifying where he was going, and you haven't heard from him in over a week. And his name is?"

"Pablo Zajalmo."

"*Vo*. Zajal*vo*," he corrected me.

"Right. Pablo Zajalvo." Oh God. I was going to butcher this and get us both killed. I just knew it. The look on Roman's face said he feared the exact same thing.

We parked, and two men in black suits slipped out of the shadows. From the looser cut of their jackets and the way they'd left them unbuttoned, I could tell they were professional guards. They greeted us as we exited the SUV.

"Identification," one requested.

Roman pulled a leather wallet out of the pocket of his shorts while I patted down my jeans, realizing I'd left my house with only my cell phone stuffed down in my front pocket.

"Shit." I shot Roman a nervous glance as the second guard tucked a hand inside the fold of his jacket.

"Civilian Jenna Skye," Roman said, nodding in my direction. "The duke requested her directly from a crime scene. There was no time to gather her personal effects."

The man touched something on his ear, and I heard a faint hum, likely from an earpiece. My senses were still in overdrive from my recent feeding, and every tiny detail seemed to overwhelm me.

Finally, the guard nodded, but he didn't take his eyes from me as they escorted us to the front door of the manor. The place was lit up, though, not as brightly as Nigel's had been. And the landscaping was clean and sharp, but not exactly decorative. This wasn't a place for parties. It was all business here.

The smell of leather and pine filled my lungs as we

stepped out of the muggy night and into a foyer lined with plush benches. Massive, framed photographs of gorgeous landscapes captured at sunrise or sunset hung on either side of a pair of French doors at the back of the foyer. Several more were spaced between arched passageways leading to other parts of the manor.

"Agents Sorano and Natani are in interrogation downstairs," one of the guards said to Roman. Roman nodded but continued to follow the man, until he stopped. "His Grace wishes to see the civilian alone."

Roman opened his mouth as if to protest, but his lips quickly snapped shut. This duke ruled with iron fangs, it seemed. I really didn't want to face him alone, but Roman had already turned and headed off toward one of the arched exits out of the foyer. He'd been an obedient servant for fifty years, and that wasn't about to change tonight.

The guard, satisfied by Roman's compliance, led me the rest of the way to the French doors. He knocked softly.

"Enter," a muffled voice called out.

The guard pushed a door open and urged me inside. "Civilian Jenna Skye, formerly a K9 officer with the St. Louis County PD," the guard announced before shutting the French doors in my face.

I blinked after him, shocked that whatever exchange he'd had with the person on the other end of his earpiece had yielded information that swiftly.

"Come closer. Let me have a look at you," the duke called from across the room.

I stole a quick glance around his office, taking in another monstrous sunset photograph and built-in bookcases, before I remembered Roman's advice and lowered my eyes to the floor. I inched forward, glancing up just enough to navigate my way to the wide desk resting like a throne at the back of the room.

"I won't bite, my dear. I assure you, I'm well fed." The comment felt like permission to look up, so I did.

I'd expected someone cold and broody, like Roman. But this man—who seemed hardly old enough for the title—was the picture of calm. His face was smooth, the soft edge of his jaw lined with a faint stubble that probably wouldn't have dissuaded an unsuspecting human from carding him at a bar. If dukes went to bars.

Chocolaty curls framed his face, adding to his boyish charm, and the inside corners of his eyebrows hitched upward, giving him a perpetual air of sympathy. He pushed up the sleeves of his white Henley and folded his hands over the top of the desk.

"Kai tells me you wish to join Blood Vice." His voice was soft and deep. It surprised me as much as his looks.

"Yes...*Your Grace*," I added, remembering Roman's

instructions.

He smiled, but I couldn't decide if it was to be pleasant or patronizing. "Your recent assistance with the serial killer case is a compelling reason for me to grant you admittance to the training program, though, a recommendation letter from your sire would be appreciated."

*Shit.*

"My sire is missing, sir." I bowed my head, hoping the statement didn't sound as damning as it felt on my lips. "And I'm very recently risen."

"How unfortunate."

"I was hoping the training program would help me acclimate, and I have a dedicated harem in place—a human and a werewolf—who are eager to join Blood Vice, too," I added since Roman wasn't there to silence me with his death glare.

The duke was quiet a moment, and I feared I'd said too much. Then he leaned back in his chair and hummed a thoughtful note.

"That's very ambitious for a vampling. But Kai is not so easily impressed, and you've already proven yourself useful." He nodded, more to himself than to me. "And we are only as strong as the team we build. Good agents are in short supply these days—humans and werewolves as much as vampires."

"Thank you, sir." I closed my eyes and soundlessly blew

out the breath I'd been holding. He hadn't exactly said yes, but it was close enough that I accepted it as such before he had a chance to offer up any doubts or criticism.

The duke picked up a pen from his desk and scribbled something in a leather-bound journal. "Leave your harem information with Belinda, and I'll have the official letters sent out by next week. The program starts the second week of September. If you have any questions about what to expect, speak with Kai."

"Thank you, Your Grace," I repeated, not knowing what else to say.

He looked up from his desk and gave me another placid smile. "You're welcome, Ms. Skye. Dismissed."

I bowed at the neck again, like Roman had said to do, and quietly exited his office. The two guards stood outside the French doors. Across the room, Roman waited on a cushioned bench near the front entrance. He stood when I approached him.

"Are you finished?" he asked, glancing over my shoulder at the guards. I could tell he wanted to ask more, but it could wait.

"I need to leave some information with…Belinda?"

Roman sighed with quiet relief, but then his head jerked up as the office doors opened behind me.

"Agent Knight," the duke called. "A word?"

Roman nodded. "Of course, Your Grace." He spared me a quick glance. "Belinda's office is in the north wing. One of the guards can direct you to it. I'll catch up with you after."

He disappeared inside the duke's office, leaving me alone in the foyer with the straight-faced guards. The one who had requested my identification pointed to the hallway branching off to my left.

"Take the stairs. First door on the right," he said.

"What, no escort?" The good news had emboldened me, and my heart felt lighter and braver.

The second guard smirked. "Everyone in this house is the duke's first line of defense. If Belinda can't handle a little green fang like you, then she doesn't belong here."

*Green fang?* I wondered if I should be insulted, but seeing as how I'd just survived my first encounter with the duke, I decided to swallow my offense and headed off to register my harem for training at the bat cave.

This was the bloody finish line, and I was going to tear through it with my head held high and still attached.

# Chapter Twenty-two

Mild, supernatural destruction was the final straw when it came to the overdue remodeling projects happening around my house. And Laura's eye for interior design was much appreciated in that regard. Left up to me, I would have restored everything to its original condition—the condition it had been in before Mom died.

"I gotta hand it to you, sis," I said, stepping back to inspect the freshly painted wall in my bathroom. "The lavender looks great in here."

"Right?" Laura finished peeling away the tape around the windowsill and beamed at me. "And it goes so well with this new vanity."

She clicked her polished nails on the marble counter laid over white drawers with silver handles. The dark-stained vanity that had been there since we were kids had made the room look small and cramped. Soaked with blood, it was even darker. Luckily, the stains had come out of the grout around the floor tiles.

Thinking of the woman whose blood I'd spent hours scrubbing out of my bathroom, I wondered what had been pulled out of her in interrogation. After relaying my harem info to Belinda the night everything happened, Kai had volunteered to drive me home, insisting Roman would be tied up for a while.

While the beefy trainer wasn't as tightlipped as Roman, he didn't offer up anything more than the press release version of the case. The two killers were part of a mutual harem, and no one was entirely certain why they were tasked with hunting vamplings. The matching bite marks on their necks gave Blood Vice something to compare to marks on staff from several clubs where vampires had gone missing, and one other human had been arrested that night for further investigation.

I had my own suspicions, but I couldn't voice them to Kai. I couldn't tell him that I was familiar with that dainty impression. That it had marred my own flesh not too long ago, though, it had since healed. I still felt it sometimes, like a hot poker in my neck, whenever I remembered the night Scarlett had taken a bite out of me.

I wanted to call Roman and talk to him about it, but I had a feeling he'd recognized the bite mark, too. And I couldn't bring myself to ask him a question I knew he'd insist was not my business.

I was just a civilian who had helped with a little undercover work. I wasn't an agent with clearance to know anything important. Not yet, anyway.

"It's about that time." Laura glanced down at her watch and sighed. "The cab should be here in ten."

I bit my bottom lip and tried to smile at her, but I couldn't. "He better be nice to you, or I'll bite his face off."

Laura's uneasy laughter let me know that she hadn't missed the literal undertone of my threat, but when I teared up, she threw her arms around me and sighed again.

"You better call me." I sobbed into her hair.

"Every day," she promised.

A second set of arms squeezed around us, and Mandy sniffled.

"I hate you," she said, squeezing until I felt a vertebra low in my back pop and Laura grunted. Duncan wriggled his way between our feet and howled a mournful tune until Mandy let go and bent down to scoop him up. She kissed the pooch between the ears and rubbed her teary cheek against his short fur. "I hope your stupid soap opera is canceled and you have to live in a cardboard box."

Laura snorted. "I love you, too."

Mandy hugged her again, squishing Duncan between their stomachs until he yipped and squirmed out of her grasp. The doorbell rang, and his little toenails skittered across the tile as he raced out of the bathroom.

"They're early," I whined. "Why is everyone so damn early all the time?"

Laura fingered her running mascara. "I'll call when my flight lands," she said to Mandy, then shot me an apologetic smile. "It will be daylight by then."

I nodded and rubbed the heel of my hand across my cheek. "I'll bug you after sunset tomorrow."

The doorbell rang again, and we all filed out of the bathroom and headed off to help Laura load up her mountain of pink, designer luggage. The porch light shone across the front lawn, and the new security light I'd installed over the garage added an extra halo of visibility. It felt necessary after the break-in, and it was also handy for other things, now that I couldn't rely on the assistance of daylight.

Collins, who had helped with the painting project, was rinsing brushes under the spigot off the front of the house. He paused to tell Laura goodbye, and to get in one last jab at her for the ogling jogging. "My eyes are up here, honey," he said, turning Laura's face nearly as red as her hair.

As the driver closed the trunk of the cab, Vin's green Volkswagen pulled into the driveway. He hopped out and gave Laura an awkward hug, wishing her a safe journey, before stepping up off the curb.

I stood in the dark with my misfit blood harem, our backs to the glowing lights coming from the house, shadows merging into one as they stretched out into the street, and waved Laura off.

My sister waved back with one of Duncan's paws, stirring a yawn from the pooch. The valium she'd slipped into a chunk of leftover hotdog for him was finally taking effect. The cab pulled away, and a few second later, Laura was gone. Out of my life and back to Tinseltown.

"Come on, kid," Collins said, nudging Mandy's shoulder. "These brushes ain't gonna wash themselves."

She grumbled but reluctantly followed him back to the spigot where our paint trays lay soaking in the grass. I'd promised her steak, cake, and cornhole shenanigans in the backyard for her help. Plus, fifty bucks. Teens were way more expensive these days.

Across the lawn, I watched Mandy *accidentally* streak a paintbrush down Collins' arm. He returned her kindness with his own brush, delivering a playful, French-glove slap across both of her cheeks. The pair of them cackled and went back to rinsing.

Vin's arms wrapped around me from behind, and he rested his chin on my shoulder. "I'm really going to miss you."

"I'll miss you, too," I said, though I wasn't sure how true that was.

Part of me wanted to love Vin, but another part of me doubted if there was a place for him in this strange new life of mine. I wondered the same thing about Collins. It had been a little too much for Laura, and I didn't blame her. At least I still had Mandy.

The girl was my saving grace. I was glad she had decided

to stick around. I knew she wasn't looking forward to being away from Serena for three whole months while we trained for Blood Vice, but we both agreed, we were in this together. I hoped Collins would come to feel the same way. I needed them, and not just for their blood.

I needed Mandy's tough determination and knowledge of this new world, and I needed Collins' human nature and link to my past. Vin was a luxury, and one I might have to give up eventually for his own good. For now, I was seeing how things played out. And I'd finally agreed to go to our ten-year class reunion with him this weekend. God help me.

The upcoming training program also meant a three-month break from Roman. Of course, I had a jump-start on that particular sabbatical. Other than the three official letters laid out on my kitchen table, I hadn't had any contact with another vampire for almost two weeks. That would all change soon.

Everything was changing, and I guessed I wanted it to, for the most part. But change, whether good or bad, was scary and uncertain. I'd been resisting it for most of my adult life. I couldn't anymore. Not if I wanted to survive. And not if I wanted to be happy.

Because I did want that. Maybe it had taken me dying to figure it out, but I wanted so desperately to be happy.

Mandy's giggle drew my attention back to the water

spigot, where she and Collins had escalated into a full-blown water fight. Mandy stuck her thumb in the end of the spigot, directing the blast in his face.

"Ceasefire! Ceasefire!" Collins pleaded, his chest heaving with laughter.

Vin kissed the side of my neck and released me. "I'm going to fire up the grill." He slipped around the opposite side of the house, fading into the shadows and narrowly avoiding becoming a casualty of the water war.

Some people just weren't cut out for battle. I would have joined in myself, but I was enjoying the truce the universe had allowed me far too much right now. I knew it wouldn't last long, but looking at the glowing faces of those who had chosen to accompany me through the darkness inspired a level of courage I hadn't felt since before my mom had died.

Dead or alive, I was going to be all right.

Catch up with Jenna and company in…

# BLOOD IN THE WATER
## BLOOD VICE BOOK THREE

### <u>Available Now!</u>

Jenna Skye and her blood harem are off to boot camp in Denver. If she can survive the three long months at the bat cave (the Blood Authority Training Center), she'll become an official Blood Vice agent. But not everyone is thrilled about the duke allowing a baby vampling to train with the big fangs, and the undead have some pretty rotten ideas when it comes to hazing.

The training program also opens Jenna's eyes to House Lilith politics, and soon she's swept away into the dark current of warring vampire families and an empire on the verge of collapse—an empire no one can know she's an heir to.

# ACKNOWLEDGMENTS

Thanks to everyone who gave Jenna Skye a chance and began this new series with me! I hope you're all having fun and warming up to the new gang I'm consorting with these days. This series is moving along a little faster than Lana Harvey's—there was a three-year gap between the first two Lana books, and only two months between Jenna's first two books. Eep! What's life without new and exhilarating challenges, right? But I hope releasing these tales a little closer together is making readers happy, because I ♥ you guys.

As always, extra thanks to my husband for keeping up with all the life things I neglected in the throes of writing; to my kiddo for the encouraging kisses and high-fives; to my sister, Justina Roquet, for being my fancy cover model; to Rebecca Frank for the fancy cover design; to Chelle Olson for making this book shine with her crazy good editing skills; to Dana Barrett for the helpful input on police lingo and protocol; to THE professor George Shelley for continuing to cheer me on—even after I ended Lana's series; to my critique group, the Four Horsemen of the Bookocalypse, who forgave me for slacking through the production of this book; and to YOU for reading it. Thank you from the bottom of my heart!

# ABOUT THE AUTHOR

*USA Today* bestselling fantasy author **Angela Roquet** is a great big weirdo. She lives in Missouri with her husband and son in a house stuffed with books, toys, skulls, owls, and glitter-speckled craft supplies. She's a member of SFWA and HWA, as well as the Four Horsemen of the Bookocalypse, her epic book critique group, where she's known as Death. When not swearing at the keyboard, she enjoys boating with her family at Lake of the Ozarks and reading books that raise eyebrows. You can find Angela online at **www.angelaroquet.com**

If you enjoyed this book, please leave a review. Your support and feedback are greatly appreciated!